To my wonderful editor, Laura McCallen, whose insight and encouragement help me make my books the best they can be. Thank you, Laura!

Kandy Shepherd swapped a career as a magazine editor for a life writing romance. She lives on a small farm in the Blue Mountains near Sydney, Australia, with her husband, daughter and lots of pets. She believes in love at first sight and real-life romance—they worked for her! Kandy loves to hear from her readers. Visit her at kandyshepherd.com.

Books by Kandy Shepherd

Mills & Boon Romance

Sydney Brides
Gift-Wrapped in Her Wedding Dress
Crown Prince's Chosen Bride

The Summer They Never Forgot
The Tycoon and the Wedding Planner
A Diamond in Her Stocking
From Paradise...to Pregnant!
Hired by the Brooding Billionaire

Visit the Author Profile page at
millsandboon.co.uk for more titles.

THE BRIDESMAID'S BABY BUMP

BY
KANDY SHEPHERD

CHAPTER ONE

ELIZA DUNNE FELT she had fallen into a fairytale as Jake Marlowe waltzed her around the vast, glittering ballroom of a medieval European castle. Hundreds of other guests whirled around them to the elegant strains of a chamber orchestra. The chatter rising and falling over the music was in a mix of languages from all around the world. Light from massive crystal chandeliers picked up the gleam of a king's ransom in jewellery and the sheen of silk in every colour of the rainbow.

Eliza didn't own any expensive jewellery. But she felt she held her own in a glamorous midnight-blue retro-style gown with a beaded bodice, nipped-in waist and full skirt, her dark hair twisted up with diamante combs, sparkling stilettos on her feet. Jake was in a tuxedo that spoke of the finest Italian tailoring.

The excitement that bubbled through her like the bubbles from expensive champagne was not from her fairytale surroundings but from her proximity to Jake. Tall, imposing, and even more handsome than the Prince whose wedding they had just witnessed, he was a man who had intrigued her from the moment she'd first met him.

Their dance was as intimate as a kiss. Eliza was intensely aware of where her body touched Jake's—his arm around her waist held her close, her hand rested on his broad shoulder, his cheek felt pleasantly rough against the smoothness of her own. She felt his warmth, breathed in his scent—spicy and fresh and utterly male—with her eyes closed, the better to savour the intoxicating effect it had on her senses. Other couples danced around them but she was scarcely aware of their presence—too lost in the rhythm of her private dance with him.

She'd first met Jake nearly two years ago, at the surprise wedding of her friend and business partner Andie Newman to *his* friend and business partner Dominic Hunt. They'd been best man and bridesmaid and had made an instant connection in an easy, friends of friends way.

She'd only seen him once since, at a business function, and they'd chatted for half the night. Eliza had relived every moment many times, unable to forget him. He'd been so unsettlingly *different*. Now they were once more best man and bridesmaid at the wedding of mutual friends.

Her other business partner, Gemma Harper, had just married Tristan, Crown Prince of Montovia. That afternoon she and Jake, as members of the bridal party, had walked slowly down the aisle of a centuries-old cathedral and watched their friends make their vows in a ceremony of almost unimaginable splendour. Now they were celebrating at a lavish reception.

She'd danced a duty dance with Tristan, then with Dominic. Jake had made his impatience obvious, then had immediately claimed her as his dance partner. The room was full of royalty and aristocrats, and Gemma had breathlessly informed her which of the men was single, but Eliza only wanted to dance with Jake. This was the first chance she'd had to spend any real time with the man who had made such a lasting impression on her.

She sighed a happy sigh, scarcely realising she'd done so.

Jake pulled away slightly and looked down at her. Her breath caught in her throat at the slow-to-ignite smile that lit his green eyes as he looked into hers. With his rumpled blond hair, strong jaw and marvellous white teeth he was as handsome as any actor or model—yet he seemed unaware of the scrutiny he got from every woman who danced by them.

'Having fun?' he asked.

Even his voice, deep and assured, sent shivers of awareness through her.

'I don't know that *fun* is quite the right word for something so spectacular. I want to rub my eyes to make sure I'm not dreaming.' She had to raise her voice over the music to be heard.

'It's extraordinary, isn't it? The over-the-top opulence of a royal wedding... It isn't something an everyday Australian guy usually gets to experience.'

Not quite an everyday guy. Eliza had to bite down on the words. At thirty-two, Jake headed his own technology solutions company and had become a billionaire while he was still in his twenties. He could probably fund an event like this with barely a blip in his bank balance. But on the two previous occasions when she'd met him, for all his wealth and brilliance and striking good looks, he had presented as notably unpretentious.

'I grew up on a sheep ranch, way out in the west

of New South Wales,' she said. 'Weddings were more often than not celebrated with a barn dance. This is the stuff of fairytales for a country girl. I've only ever seen rooms like this in a museum.'

'You seem like a sophisticated city girl to me. Boss of the best party-planning business in Sydney.' Jake's green eyes narrowed as he searched her face. 'The loveliest of the Party Queens.' His voice deepened in tone.

'Thank you,' she said, preening a little at his praise, fighting a blush because he'd called her lovely. 'I'm not the boss, though. Andie, Gemma and I are equal partners in Party Queens.'

Eliza was Business Director, Andie looked after design and Gemma the food.

'The other two are savvy, but you're the business brains,' he said. 'There can be no doubt about that.'

'I guess I am,' she said.

She was not being boastful in believing that the success of Party Queens owed a lot to her sound financial management. The business was everything to her and she'd given her life to it since it had launched three years ago.

'Tristan told me Gemma organised the wedding herself,' Jake said. 'With some long-distance help from you and Andie.'

'True,' said Eliza.

Jake—the 'everyday Aussie guy'—was good friends with the Prince. They'd met, he'd told her, on the Montovian ski-fields years ago.

'Apparently the courtiers were aghast at her audacity in breaking with tradition.'

'Yet look how brilliantly it turned out—another success for Party Queens. My friend the Crown Princess.'

Eliza shook her head in proud wonderment. 'One day she'll be a real queen. But for Gemma it isn't about the royal trappings, you know. It's all about being with Tristan—she's so happy, so in love.'

Eliza couldn't help the wistful note that crept into her voice. That kind of happiness wasn't for her. Of course she'd started out wanting the happy-ever-after love her friends had found. But it had proved elusive. So heartbreakingly elusive that, at twenty-nine, she had given up on hoping it would ever happen. She had a broken marriage behind her, and nothing but dating disasters since her divorce. No way would she get married again. She would not risk being trapped with a domineering male like her ex-husband, like her father. Being single was a state that suited her, even if she did get lonely sometimes.

'Tristan is happy too,' said Jake. 'He credits me for introducing him to his bride.'

Jake had recommended Party Queens to his friend the Crown Prince when Tristan had had to organise an official function in Sydney. Tristan had been incognito when Gemma had met him and they'd fallen in love. The resulting publicity had been off the charts for Party Queens, and Eliza would always be grateful to Jake for putting the job their way.

Jake looked down into her face. 'But you're worried about what Gemma's new status means for your business, aren't you?'

'How did you know that?' she asked, a frown pleating her forehead.

'One business person gets to read the signs in another,' he said. 'It was the way you frowned when I mentioned Gemma's name.'

'I didn't think I was so transparent,' she said, and realised she'd frowned again. 'Yes, I admit I *am* concerned. Gemma wants to stay involved with the business, but I don't know how that can work with her fifteen thousand kilometres away from our headquarters.' She looked around her. 'She's moved into a different world and has a whole set of new royal duties to master.'

Eliza knew it would be up to her to solve the problem. Andie and Gemma were the creatives; she was the worrier, the plotter, the planner. The other two teased her that she was a control freak, let her know when she got too bossy, but the three Party Queens complemented each other perfectly.

Jake's arm tightened around her waist. 'Don't let your concern ruin the evening for you. I certainly don't want to let it ruin mine.'

His voice was deep and strong and sent a thrill of awareness coursing through her.

'You're right. I just want to enjoy every moment of this,' she said.

Every moment with him. She closed her eyes in bliss when he tightened his arms around her as they danced. He was the type of man she had never dreamed existed.

The Strauss waltz came to an end. 'More champagne?' Jake asked. 'We could drink it out on the terrace.'

'Excellent idea,' she said, her heart pounding a little harder at the prospect of being alone with him.

The enclosed terrace ran the length of the ballroom, with vast arched windows looking out on the view across the lit-up castle gardens to the lake, where a huge pale moon rode high in the sky. Beyond the lake were snow-capped mountains, only a ghostly hint of their peaks to be seen under the dim light from the moon.

There was a distinct October chill to the Montovian air. It seemed quite natural for Jake to put his arm around her as Eliza gazed out at the view. She welcomed his warmth, still hyper-aware of his touch as she leaned close to his hard strength. There must be a lot of honed muscle beneath that tuxedo.

'This place hardly seems real,' she said, keeping her voice low in a kind of reverence.

'Awesome in the true sense of the word,' he said.

Eliza sipped slowly from the flute of champagne. Wine was somewhat of a hobby for her, and she knew this particular vintage was the most expensive on the planet, its cost per bubble astronomical. She had consulted with Gemma on the wedding wine list. But she was too entranced with Jake to be really aware of what she was drinking. It might have been lemon soda for all the attention she paid it.

He took the glass from her hand and placed it on an antique table nearby. Then he slid her around so she faced him. He was tall—six foot four, she guessed—and she was glad she was wearing stratospheric heels. She didn't like to feel at a disadvantage with a man—even this man.

'I've waited all day for us to be alone,' he said.

'Me too,' she said, forcing the tremor out of her voice.

How alone? She had a luxurious guest apartment in the castle all to herself, where they could truly be by themselves. No doubt Jake had one the same.

He looked into her face for a long moment, so close

she could feel his breath stir her hair. His eyes seemed to go a deeper shade of green. *He was going to kiss her.* She found her lips parting in anticipation of his touch as she swayed towards him. There was nothing she wanted more at this moment than to be kissed by Jake Marlowe.

Yet she hesitated. Whether she called it the elephant in the room, or the poisoned apple waiting to be offered as in the fairytale, there was something they had not talked about all day in the rare moments when they had been alone. Something that had to be said.

With a huge effort of will she stepped back, folded her arms in front of her chest, took a deep breath. 'Jake, has anything changed since we last spoke at Tristan's party in Sydney? Is your divorce through?'

He didn't immediately reply, and her heart sank to the level of her sparkling shoes. 'Yes, to your first question. Divorce proceedings are well under way. But to answer your second question: it's not final yet. I'm still waiting on the decree nisi, let alone the decree absolute.'

'Oh.' It was all she could manage as disappointment speared through her. 'I thought—'

'You thought I'd be free by now?' he said gruffly.

She chewed her lip and nodded. There was so much neither of them dared say. Undercurrents pulled them in the direction of possibilities best left unspoken. Such as what might happen between them if he wasn't still legally married...

It was his turn to frown. 'So did I. But it didn't work out like that. The legalities... The property settlements...'

'Of course,' she said.

So when will *you be free?* She swallowed the words before she could give impatient voice to them.

He set his jaw. 'I'm frustrated about it, but it's complex.'

Millions of dollars and a life together to be dismantled. Eliza knew all about the legal logistics of that, but on a much smaller scale. There were joint assets to be divided. Then there were emotions, all twisted and tangled throughout a marriage of any duration, that had to be untangled—and sometimes torn. Wounds. Scars. All intensely personal. She didn't feel she could ask him any more.

During their first meeting Jake had told her his wife of seven years wanted a divorce but he didn't. At their second meeting he'd said the divorce was underway. Eliza had sensed he was ambivalent about it, so had declined his suggestion that they keep in touch. Her attraction to him was too strong for her ever to pretend she could be 'just friends' with him. She'd want every chance to act on that attraction.

But she would not date a married man. She wouldn't kiss a married man. Even when he was nearly divorced. Even when he was Jake Marlowe. No way did she want to be caught up in any media speculation about being 'the other woman' in his divorce. And then there was the fact that her ex had cheated on her towards the end of their marriage. She didn't know Jake's wife. But she wouldn't want to cause her the same kind of pain.

Suffocating with disappointment, Eliza stepped back from him. She didn't have expectations of any kind of relationship with him—just wanted a chance to explore the surprising connection between them. Starting with a kiss. Then...? Who knew?

She cleared her throat. 'I wish—' she started to say.

But then an alarm started beeping, shrill and intrusive. Startled, she jumped.

Jake glanced down at his watch, swore under his breath. 'Midnight,' he said. 'I usually call Australia now, for a business catch-up.' He switched off the alarm. 'But not tonight.'

It seemed suddenly very quiet on the terrace, with only faint strains of music coming from the ballroom, distant laughter from a couple at the other end of the terrace. Eliza was aware of her own breathing and the frantic pounding of her heart.

'No. Make your call. It's late. I have to go.'

She doubted he'd guessed the intensity of her disappointment, how much she'd had pinned on this meeting—and she didn't want him to see it on her face. She turned, picked up her long, full skirts and prepared to run.

Then Jake took hold of her arm and pulled her back to face him. 'Don't go, Eliza. Please.'

Jake watched as Eliza struggled to contain her disappointment. She seemed to pride herself on having a poker face. But her feelings were only too apparent to him. And her disappointment had nothing on his.

'But I have to go,' she said as she tried to pull away from him. 'You're still married. We can't—'

'Act on the attraction that's been there since the get go?'

Mutely, she nodded.

Their first meeting had been electric—an instant *something* between them. For him it had been a revelation. A possibility of something new and exciting beyond the dead marriage he had been struggling to revive. Eliza had been so beautiful, so smart, so interesting—yet so unattainable. The second time they'd met he'd realised the attraction was mutual. And tonight he'd sensed in her the same longing for more that he felt.

But it was still not their time to explore it. She'd made it very clear the last time they'd met that she could not be friends with a married man—and certainly not more than friends. He'd respected her stance. As a wealthy man he'd met more than a few women with dollar signs flashing in their eyes who had held no regard for a man's wedding vows—or indeed their own.

When Tristan had asked him to be best man at his wedding he'd said yes straight away. The bonus had been a chance to see Eliza again. In her modest lavender dress she'd been the loveliest of the bridesmaids, eclipsing—at least in his admittedly biased eyes—even the bride. Tonight, in a formal gown that showed off her tiny waist and feminine curves, she rivalled any of the royalty in the ballroom.

'This is not what I'd hoped for this evening,' he said.

'Me neither.' Her voice was barely louder than a whisper as she looked up to him.

He caught his breath at how beautiful she was. Her eyes were a brilliant blue that had him struggling to describe them—like sapphires was the closest he could come. They were framed by brows and lashes as black as her hair, in striking contrast to her creamy skin. Irish colouring, he suspected. He knew nothing about her heritage, very little about her.

Jake thirsted to know more.

He—a man who had thought he could never be interested in another woman. Who had truly thought he had married for life. He'd been so set on hanging on to his marriage to a woman who didn't want to be married any more—who had long outgrown him and he her—that he hadn't let himself think of any other. Until he'd met Eliza. And seen hope for the future.

He cursed the fact that the divorce process was taking so long. At first he'd delayed it because he'd hoped he could work things out with his soon-to-be ex-wife. Even though she'd had become virtually a stranger to him. Then he'd discovered how she'd betrayed him. Now he was impatient to have it settled, all ties severed.

'A few months and I'll be free. It's so close, Eliza. In fact it's debatable that I'm not single again already. It's just a matter of a document. Couldn't we—?'

He could see her internal debate, the emotions flitting across her face. Was pleased to see that anticipation was one of them. But he was not surprised when she shook her head.

'No,' she said, in a voice that wasn't quite steady. 'Not until you're legally free. Not until we can see each other with total honesty.'

How could he fault her argument? He admired her integrity. Although he groaned his frustration. Not with her, but with the situation.

He pulled her close in a hug. It was difficult not to turn it into something more, not to tilt her face up to his and kiss her. A campaign of sensual kisses and subtle caresses might change her mind—he suspected she wanted him as much as he wanted her. But she was right. He wasn't ready—in more ways than one.

'As soon as the divorce is through I'll get in touch,

come see you in Sydney.' He lived in Brisbane, the capital city of Queensland, about an hour's flight north.

Scarcely realising he was doing so, he stroked the smooth skin of her bare shoulders, her exposed back. It was a gesture more of reassurance than anything overtly sexual. He couldn't let himself think about Eliza and sex. Not now. Not yet. Or he'd go crazy.

Her head was nestled against his shoulder and he felt her nod. 'I'd like that,' she said, her voice muffled.

He held her close for a long, silent moment. Filled his senses with her sweet floral scent, her warmth. Wished he didn't have to let her go. Then she pulled away. Looked up at him. Her cheeks were flushed pink, which intensified the blue of her eyes.

'I've been in Montovia for a week. I fly out to Sydney tomorrow morning. I won't see you again,' she said.

'I have meetings in Zurich,' he said. 'I'll be gone very early.'

'So...so this is goodbye,' she said.

He put his fingers to the soft lushness of her mouth. 'Until next time,' he said.

For a long moment she looked up at him, searching his face with those remarkable eyes. Then she nodded. 'Until next time.'

Without another word Eliza turned away from him and walked away down the long enclosed terrace that ran along the outside of the ballroom. She did not turn back.

Jake watched her. Her back was held erect, the full skirts of her deep blue dress with its elaborately beaded bodice nipped into her tiny waist swishing around her at each step. He watched her until she turned to the right through an archway. Still she didn't look back, although he had his hand ready to wave farewell to her. Then she disappeared out of sight.

She left behind her just the lingering trace of her scent. He breathed it in to capture its essence. Took a step to go after her, then halted himself. He had no right to call her back a second time. He groaned and slammed his hand against the ancient stone wall.

For a long time he looked out through the window to the still lake beyond. Then he looked back to the ballroom. Without Eliza to dance with there was no point in returning. Besides, he felt like an impostor among the glittering throng. His role as best man, as friend to the Prince, gave him an entrée to their world. His multi-million-dollar houses and string of prestige European cars made him look the part.

Would they welcome him so readily into their elite company if they knew the truth about his past? Would Eliza find him so appealing if she knew his secrets?

He took out his phone and made his business call, in desperate need of distraction.

CHAPTER TWO

Six months later

ELIZA NOTICED JAKE MARLOWE the instant he strode into the business class lounge at Sydney's Kingsford Smith Airport. Tall, broad-shouldered, with a surfer's blond hair and tan, his good looks alone would attract attention. The fact that he was a billionaire whose handsome face was often in the media guaranteed it. Heads turned discreetly as he made his way with his easy, athletic stride towards the coffee station.

He was half a room away from her, but awareness tingled down Eliza's spine. A flush of humiliation warmed her cheeks. She hadn't seen him or heard from him since the wedding in Montovia, despite his promise to get in touch when his divorce was through. And here he was—on his way out of Sydney.

Jake had been in her hometown for heaven knew how long and hadn't cared to get in touch. She thought of a few choice names for him but wouldn't let herself mutter them, even under her breath. Losing her dignity over him was not worth it.

Over the last months she'd gone past disappointed, through angry, to just plain embarrassed that she'd believed him. That she'd allowed herself to spin hopes and dreams around seeing him again—finally being able to act on that flare of attraction between them. An attraction that, despite her best efforts to talk herself out of it, had flamed right back to life at the sight of him. She'd failed dismally in her efforts to extinguish it. He looked just as good in faded jeans and black T-shirt as he looked in a tuxedo. Better, perhaps. Every hot hunk sensor in her body alerted her to that.

But good looks weren't everything. She'd kidded herself that Jake was something he wasn't. Sure, they'd shared some interesting conversations, come close to a kiss. But when it boiled down to it, it appeared he was a slick tycoon who'd known how to spin the words he'd thought would please her. And she'd been sucker enough to fall for it. Had there been *anything* genuine about him?

Jake had put her through agony by not getting in touch when he'd said he would. She never wanted that kind of emotional turmoil in her life again. Especially not now, when Party Queens was in possible peril. She needed all her wits about her to ensure the future of the company that had become her life.

Perhaps back then she'd been convenient for Jake—the bridesmaid paired with the best man. An instant temporary couple. Now he was single and oh-so-eligible he must have women flinging themselves at him from all sides. Even now, as she sneaked surreptitious glances at him, a well-dressed woman edged up close to him, smiling up into his face.

Jake laughed at something she said. Eliza's senses jolted into hyper mode. *He looked so handsome when he laughed*. Heck, he looked so handsome whatever he did.

Darn her pesky libido. Her brain could analyse exactly what she didn't want in a man, but then her body argued an opposing message. She'd let her libido take over at Gemma's wedding, when she'd danced with Jake and let herself indulge in a fantasy that there could be something between them one day. But she prided herself on her self-control. Eliza allowed herself a moment to let her eyes feast on him, in the same way she would a mouthwatering treat she craved but was forbidden to have. Then she ducked her head and hid behind the pale pink pages of her favourite financial newspaper.

Perhaps she hadn't ducked fast enough—perhaps she hadn't masked the hunger in her gaze as successfully as she'd thought. Or perhaps Jake had noticed her when he came in as readily as she had noticed him.

Just moments later she was aware of him standing in front of her, legs braced in a way that suggested he wasn't going anywhere. Her heart started to thud at a million miles an hour. As she lowered the newspaper and looked up at him she feigned surprise. But the expression in his green eyes told her she hadn't fooled him one little bit.

She gathered all her resolve to school her face into a mask of polite indifference. He could not know how much he'd hurt her. Not *hurt*. That gave him too much power. *Offended*. His divorce had been splashed all over the media for the last three months. Yet there'd been no phone call from him. What a fool she'd been to have expected one. She'd obviously read way too much into that memorable 'next time' farewell.

Eliza went to get up but he sat down in the vacant seat next to her and angled his body towards her. In doing so he brushed his knee against her thigh, and she tried desperately not to gasp at his touch. Her famed self-control seemed to wobble every which way when she found herself within touching distance of Jake Marlowe.

He rested his hands on his thighs, which brought them too close for comfort. She refused to let herself think about how good they'd felt on her body in that close embrace of their dance. She could not let herself be blinded by physical attraction to the reality of this man.

'Eliza,' he said.

'Jake,' she said coolly, with a nod of acknowledgment.

She crossed her legs to break contact with his. Made a show of folding her newspaper, its rustle satisfyingly loud in the silence between them.

There was a long, awkward pause. She had no intention of helping him out by being the first one to dive into conversation. Not when he'd treated her with such indifference. Surely the thread of friendship they'd established had entitled her to better.

She could see he was looking for the right words, and at any other time she might have felt sorry for this intelligent, successful man who appeared to be struggling to make conversation. Would have fed him words to make it easier for him. But she knew how articulate Jake could be. How he had charmed her. This sudden shyness must be all part of his game. It seemed he felt stymied at seeing her by accident when he'd so obviously not wanted to see her by intent.

She really should hold her tongue and let him stumble through whatever he had to say. But she knew there wasn't much time before her flight would be called. And this might be her only chance to call him on the way he had broken his promise.

Of course it hadn't been a *promise* as such. But, spellbound by the magic of that royal wedding in Montovia, she had believed every word about there being a 'next time', when he was free. She'd never believed in fairytales—but she'd believed in *him*.

Even though the lounge chairs were spaced for privacy in the business class lounge—not crammed on top of each other like at the airport gate, where she was accustomed to waiting for a flight—she was aware that she and Jake were being observed and might possibly be overheard. She would have to be discreet.

She leaned closer to him and spoke in an undertone. 'So whatever happened to getting in touch? I see from the media that your divorce is well and truly done and delivered. You're now considered to be the most eligible bachelor in the country. You must be enjoying that.'

Jake shifted in his seat. Which brought his thigh back in touch with her knee. She pointedly crossed her legs again to break the contact. It was way too distracting.

'You couldn't be more wrong.' He cleared his throat. 'I want to explain.'

Eliza didn't want to hear his half-hearted apologies. She glanced at her watch. 'I don't think so. My flight is about to be called.'

'So is mine. Where are you headed?'

It would be childish to spit, *None of your business*, so she refrained. 'Port Douglas.'

She'd been counting the days until she could get

up to the resort in far north-east tropical Queensland. From Sydney she was flying to Cairns, the nearest airport. She needed to relax—to get away from everyday distractions so she could get her head around what she needed to do to ensure Party Queens' ongoing success.

Jake's expression, which had bordered on glum, brightened perceptibly. 'Are you on Flight 321 to Cairns? So am I.'

Eliza felt the colour drain from her face. It couldn't be. It just *couldn't* be. Australia was an enormous country. Yet she happened to be flying to the same destination as Jake Marlowe. What kind of cruel coincidence was that?

'Yes,' she said through gritted teeth.

Port Douglas was a reasonably sized town. The resort she was booked into was pretty much self-contained. She would make darn sure she didn't bump into him.

Just then they called the flight. She went to rise from her seat. Jake put his hand on her arm to detain her. She flinched.

He spoke in a fierce undertone. 'Please, Eliza. I know it was wrong of me not to have got in touch as I said I would. But I had good reason.'

She stared at him, uncertain whether or not to give him the benefit of the doubt. He seemed so sincere. But then he'd seemed so sincere at the wedding. Out there on the terrace, in a place and at a time that hardly seemed real any more. As if it *had* been a fairytale. How could she believe a word he said?

'A phone call to explain would have sufficed. Even a text.'

'That wouldn't have worked. I want you to hear me out.'

There was something about his request that was difficult to resist. She wanted to hear what he had to say. Out of curiosity, if nothing else. Huh! Who was she kidding? How could she *not* want to hear what he had to say? After six months of wondering why the deafening silence?

She relented. 'Perhaps we could meet for a coffee in Port Douglas.' At a café. Not her room. Or his. For just enough time to hear his explanation. Then she could put Jake Marlowe behind her.

'How are you getting to Port Douglas from Cairns?' he asked.

'I booked a shuttle bus from the airport to the resort.'

His eyebrows rose in such disbelief it forced from her a reluctant smile.

'Yes, a shuttle bus. It's quite comfortable—and so much cheaper than a taxi for an hour-long trip. That's how we non-billionaires travel. I'm flying economy class, too.'

When she'd first started studying in Sydney, cut off from any family support because she'd refused to toe her father's line, she'd had to budget for every cent. It was a habit she'd kept. Why waste money on a business class seat for a flight of less than three hours?

'Then why...?' He gestured around him at the exclusive waiting area.

'I met a friend going through Security. She invited me in here on her guest pass. She went out on an earlier flight.'

'Lucky for me—otherwise I might have missed you.'

She made a *humph* kind of sound at that, which drew a half-smile from him.

'Contrary to what you might think, I'm very glad to see you,' he said, in that deep, strong voice she found so very appealing.

'That's good to hear,' she said, somewhat mollified. Of course she was glad to see him too—in spite of her better judgement. How could she deny even to herself that her every sense was zinging with awareness of him? She would have to be very careful not to be taken in by him again.

'Are you going to Port Douglas on business or pleasure?'

'Pleasure,' she said, without thinking. Then regretted her response as a flush reddened on her cheeks.

She had fantasised over pleasure with *him*. When it came to Jake Marlowe it wasn't so easy to switch off the attraction that had been ignited at their very first meeting. She would have to fight very hard against it.

It had taken some time to get her life to a steady state after her divorce, and she didn't want it tipping over again. When she'd seen the media reports of Jake's divorce, but hadn't heard from him, she'd been flung back to a kind of angst she didn't welcome. She cringed when she thought about how often she'd checked her phone for a call that had never come. It wasn't a situation where she might have called *him*. And she hated not being in control—of her life, her emotions. Never did she want to give a man that kind of power over her.

'I mean relaxation,' she added hastily. 'Yes, relaxation.'

'Party Queens keeping you busy?'

'Party Queens always keeps me busy. Too busy right

now. That's why I'm grabbing the chance for a break. I desperately need some time away from the office.'

'Have you solved the Gemma problem?'

'No. I need to give it more thought. Gemma will always be a director of Party Queens, for as long as the company exists. It's just that—'

'Can passengers Dunne and Marlowe please make their way to Gate Eleven, where their flight is ready for departure?'

The voice boomed over the intercom.

Eliza sat up abruptly, her newspaper falling in a flurry of pages to the floor. Hissed a swearword under her breath. 'We've got to get going. I don't want to miss that plane.'

'How about I meet you at the other end and drive you to Port Douglas?'

Eliza hated being late. For anything. Flustered, she hardly heard him. 'Uh...okay,' she said, not fully aware of what she might be letting herself in for. 'Let's go!'

She grabbed her wheel-on cabin bag—her only luggage—and half-walked, half-ran towards the exit of the lounge.

Jake quickly caught up and led the way to the gate. Eliza had to make a real effort to keep up with his long stride. They made the flight with only seconds to spare. There was no time to say anything else as she breathlessly boarded the plane through the cattle class entrance while Jake headed to the pointy end up front.

Jake had a suspicion that Eliza might try to avoid him at Cairns airport. As soon as the flight landed he called through to the garage where he kept his car to have it brought round. Having had the advantage of being the first to disembark, he was there at the gate to head Eliza off.

She soon appeared, head down, intent, so didn't see him as he waited for her. The last time he'd seen her she'd been resplendent in a ballgown. Now she looked just as good, in cut-off skinny pants that showed off her pert rear end and slim legs, topped with a form-fitting jacket. Deep blue again. She must like that colour. Her dark hair was pulled back in a high ponytail. She might travel Economy but she would look right at home in First Class.

For a moment he regretted the decision he'd made to keep her out of his life. Three months wasted in an Eliza-free zone. But the aftermath of his divorce had made him unfit for female company. Unfit for *any* company, if truth be told.

He'd been thrown so badly by the first big failure of his life that he'd gone completely out of kilter. Drunk too much. Made bad business decisions that had had serious repercussions to his bottom line. Mistakes he'd had to do everything in his power to fix. He had wealth, but it would never be enough to blot out the poverty of his childhood, to assuage the hunger for more that had got him into such trouble. He had buried himself in his work, determined to reverse the wrong turns he'd made. But he hadn't been able to forget Eliza.

'Eliza!' he called now.

She started, looked up, was unable to mask a quick flash of guilt.

'Jake. Hi.'

Her voice was higher than usual. Just as sweet, but strained. She was not a good liar. He stored that information up for later, as he did in his assessments of clients. He'd learned young that knowledge of people's weaknesses was a useful tool. Back then it had been for survival. Now it was to give him a competitive advantage and keep him at the top. He could not let himself slide again.

'I suspected you might try and avoid me, so I decided to head you off at the pass,' he said.

Eliza frowned unconvincingly. 'Why would you do that?'

'Because you obviously think I'm a jerk for not calling you after the divorce. I'm determined to change your mind.' He didn't want to leave things the way they were. Not when thoughts of her had intruded, despite his best efforts to forget her.

'Oh,' she said, after a long pause. 'You could do that over coffee. Not during an hour's drive to Port Douglas.'

So she'd been mulling over the enforced intimacy of a journey in his car. So had he. But to different effect.

'How do you know I won't need an hour with you?'

She shrugged slender shoulders. 'I guess I don't. But I've booked the shuttle bus. The driver is expecting me.'

'Call them and cancel.' He didn't want to appear too high-handed. But no way was she going to get on that shuttle bus. 'Come on, Eliza. It will be much more comfortable in my car.'

'Your rental car?'

'I have a house in Port Douglas. And a car.'

'I thought you lived in Brisbane?'

'I do. The house in Port Douglas is an escape house.'

He took hold of her wheeled bag. 'Do you need to pick up more luggage?'

She shook her head. 'This is all I have. A few biki-nis and sundresses is all I need for four days.'

Jake forced himself not to think how Eliza would look in a bikini. She was wearing flat shoes and he re-alised how petite she was. Petite, slim, but with curves in all the right places. She would look sensational in a bikini.

'My car is out front. Let's go.'

Still she hesitated. 'So you'll drop me at my resort hotel?'

Did she think he was about to abduct her? It wasn't such a bad idea, if that was what it took to get her to listen to him. 'Your private driver—at your service,' he said with a mock bow.

She smiled that curving smile he found so delight-ful. The combination of astute businesswoman and quick-to-laughter Party Queen was part of her appeal.

'Okay, I accept the offer,' she said.

The warm midday air hit him as they left the air-conditioning of the terminal. Eliza shrugged off her jacket to reveal a simple white top that emphasised the curves of her breasts. She stretched out her slim, toned arms in a movement he found incredibly sensual, as if she were welcoming the sun to her in an embrace.

'Nice and hot,' she said with a sigh of pleasure. 'Just what I want. Four days of relaxing and swimming and eating great food.'

'April is a good time of year here,' he said. 'Less chance of cyclone and perfect conditions for diving on the Great Barrier Reef.'

The garage attendant had brought Jake's new-model four-by-four to the front of the airport. It was a lux-ury to keep a car for infrequent use. Just as it was to keep a house up here that was rarely used. But he liked being able to come and go whenever he wanted. It had been his bolthole through the unhappiest times of his marriage.

'Nice car,' Eliza said.

Jake remembered they'd talked about cars at their first meeting. He'd been impressed by how knowledge-able she was. Face it—he'd been impressed by *her*. Period. No wonder she'd been such a difficult woman to forget.

He put her bag into the back, went to help her up into the passenger's seat, but she had already swung herself effortlessly up. He noticed the sleek muscles in her arms and legs. Exercise was a non-negotiable part of her day, he suspected. Everything about her spoke of discipline and control. He wondered how it would be to see her come to pieces with pleasure in his arms.

Jake settled himself into the driver's seat. 'Have you been to Port Douglas before?' he asked.

'Yes, but not for some time,' she said. 'I loved it and always wanted to come back. But there's been no time for vacations. As you know, Party Queens took off quickly. It's an intense, people-driven business. I can't be away from it for long. But I need to free my head to think about how we can make it work with Gemma not on the ground.'

Can't or *didn't want to* be away from her job? Jake had recognised a fellow workaholic when he'd first met her.

'So you're familiar with the drive from Cairns to Port Douglas?'

With rainforest on one side and the sea on the other,

it was considered one of the most scenic drives in Australia.

'I planned the timing of my flight to make sure I saw it in daylight.'

'I get the feeling very little is left to chance with you, Eliza.'

'You've got it,' she said with a click of her fingers. 'I plan, schedule, timetable and organise my life to the minute.'

She was the total opposite of his ex-wife. In looks, in personality, in attitude. The two women could not be more different.

'You don't like surprises?' he asked.

'Surprises have a habit of derailing one's life.'

She stilled, almost imperceptibly, and there was a slight hitch to her voice that made him wonder about the kind of surprises that had hit her.

'I like things to be on track. For me to be at the wheel.'

'So by hijacking you I've ruined your plans for today?'

His unwilling passenger shrugged slender shoulders.

'Just a deviation. I'm still heading for my resort. It will take the same amount of time. Just a different mode of transportation.' She turned her head to face him. 'Besides. I'm on vacation. From schedules and routine as much as from anything else.'

Eliza reached back and undid the tie from her ponytail, shook out her hair so it fell in a silky mass to her shoulders. With her hair down she looked even lovelier. Younger than her twenty-nine years. More relaxed. He'd like to run his hands through that hair, bunch it back from her face to kiss her. Instead he

tightened his hands on the steering wheel as she settled back in her seat.

'When you're ready to tell me why I had to read
about your divorce in the gossip columns rather than
hear it from you,' she said, 'I'm all ears.'

CHAPTER THREE

JAKE WAS VERY good at speaking the language of computers and coding. At talking the talk when it came to commercial success. While still at university he had come up with a concept for ground-breaking software tools to streamline the digital workflow of large businesses. His friend Dominic Hunt had backed him. The resulting success had made a great deal of money for both young men. And Jake had continued on a winning streak that had made him a billionaire.

But for all his formidable skills Jake wasn't great at talking about emotions. At admitting that he had fears and doubts. Or conceding to any kind of failure. It was one of the reasons he'd got into such trouble when he was younger. Why he'd fallen apart after the divorce. No matter how much he worked on it, he still considered it a character flaw.

He hoped he'd be able to make a good fist of explaining to Eliza why he hadn't got in touch until now.

He put the four-by-four into gear and headed for the Captain Cook Highway to Port Douglas. Why they called it a highway, he'd never know—it was a narrow two-lane road in most places. To the left was dense vegetation, right back to the distant hills. To the right was the vastness of the Pacific Ocean, its turquoise sea bounded by narrow, deserted beaches, broken by small islands. In places the road ran almost next to the sand. He'd driven along this road many times, but never failed to be impressed by the grandeur of the view.

He didn't look at Eliza but kept his eyes on the road. 'I'll cut straight to it,' he said. 'I want to apologise for not getting in touch when I said I would. I owe you an explanation.'

'Fire away,' Eliza said.

Her voice was cool. The implication? *This had better be good.*

He swallowed hard. 'The divorce eventually came through three months ago.'

'I heard. Congratulations.'

He couldn't keep the cynical note from his voice. 'You *congratulate* me. Lots of people congratulated me. A divorce party was even suggested. To celebrate my freedom from the ball and chain.'

'Party Queens has organised a few divorce parties. They're quite a thing these days.'

'Not *my* thing,' he said vehemently. 'I didn't want congratulations. Or parties to celebrate what I saw as a failure. The end of something that didn't work.'

'Was that because you were still...still in love with your wife?'

A quick glance showed Eliza had a tight grip on the red handbag she held on her lap. He hated talking about stuff like this. Even after all he'd worked on in the last months.

'No. There hadn't been any love there for a long

time. It ended with no anger or animosity. Just indifference. Which was almost worse.'

He'd met his ex when they were both teenagers. They'd dated on and off over the early years. Marriage had felt inevitable. He'd changed a lot; she hadn't wanted change. Then she'd betrayed him. He'd loved her. It had hurt.

'That must have been traumatic in its own way.' Eliza's reply sounded studiously neutral.

'More traumatic than I could have imagined. The process dragged on for too long.'

'It must have been a relief when it was all settled.'

Again he read the subtext to her sentence: *All settled, but you didn't call me.* It hinted at a hurt she couldn't mask. Hurt caused by *him.* He had to make amends.

'I didn't feel relief. I felt like I'd been turned upside down and wasn't sure where I'd landed. Couldn't find my feet. My ex and I had been together off and on for years, married for seven. Then I was on my own. It wasn't just her I'd lost. It was a way of life.'

'I understand that,' she said.

The shadow that passed across her face hinted at unspoken pain. She'd gone through divorce too. Though she hadn't talked much about it on the previous occasions when they had met.

He dragged in a deep breath. *Spit it out. Get this over and done with.* 'It took a few wipe-out weeks at work for me to realise going out and drinking wasn't the way to deal with it.'

'It usually isn't,' she said.

He was a guy. A tough, successful guy. To him, being

unable to cope with loss was a sign of weakness. Weakness he wasn't genetically programmed to admit to. But the way he'd fallen to pieces had lost him money. That couldn't be allowed to happen again.

'Surely you had counselling?' she said. 'I did after my divorce. It helped.'

'Guys like me don't do counselling.'

'You bottle it all up inside you instead?'

'Something like that.'

'That's not healthy—it festers,' she said. 'Not that it's any of my business.'

The definitive turning point in his life had not been his divorce. That had come much earlier, when he'd been aged fifteen, angry and rebellious. He'd been forced to face up to the way his life was going, the choices he would have to make. To take one path or another.

Jake didn't know how much Eliza knew about Dominic's charity—The Underground Help Centre in Brisbane for homeless young people—or Jake's involvement in it. A social worker with whom both Dominic and Jake had crossed paths headed the charity. Jim Hill had helped Jake at a time when he'd most needed it. He had become a friend. Without poking or prying, he had noticed Jake's unexpected devastation after his marriage break-up, and pointed him in the right direction for confidential help.

'Someone told me about a support group for divorced guys,' Jake said, with a quick, sideways glance to Eliza and in a tone that did not invite further questions.

'That's good,' she said with an affirmative nod.

He appreciated that she didn't push it. He still choked at the thought he'd had to seek help.

The support group had been exclusive, secret, limited to a small number of elite men rich enough to pay the stratospheric fees. Men who wanted to protect their wealth in the event of remarriage, who needed strategies to avoid the pitfalls of dating after divorce. Jake had wanted to know how to barricade his heart as well as his bank balance.

The men and the counsellors had gone into lockdown for a weekend at a luxury retreat deep in the rainforest. It had been on a first-name-only basis, but Jake had immediately recognised some of the high-profile men. No doubt they had recognised him too. But they had proved to be discreet.

'Men don't seem to seek help as readily as women,' Eliza said.

'It was about dealing with change more than anything,' he said.

'Was that why you didn't get in touch?' she said, with an edge to her voice. 'You changed your mind?'

Jake looked straight ahead at the road. 'I wasn't ready for another relationship. I needed to learn to live alone. That meant no dating. In particular not dating *you*.'

Her gasp told him how much he'd shocked her.

'*Me?* Why?'

'From the first time we met you sparked something that told me there could be life after divorce. I could see myself getting serious about you. I don't want serious. But I couldn't get you out of my head. I had to see you again.'

To be sure she was real and not some fantasy that had built up in his mind.

* * *

Eliza didn't even notice the awesome view of the ocean that stretched as far as the eye could see. Or the sign indicating the turn-off to a crocodile farm that would normally make her shudder. All she was aware of was Jake. She stared at him.

'*Serious?* But we hardly knew each other. Did you think I had my life on hold until you were free so I could bolt straight into a full-on relationship?'

Jake took his eyes off the road for a second to glance at her. 'Come on, Eliza. There was something there between us. Something more than a surface attraction. Something we both wanted to act on.'

'Maybe,' she said.

Of course there had been something there. But she wasn't sure she wanted to admit to it. Not when she'd spent all that time trying to suppress it. Not when it had the potential to hurt her. Those three months of seeing his divorce splashed over the media, of speculation on who might hook up with the billionaire bachelor had hurt. He had said he'd get in touch. Then he hadn't. How could she trust his word again? She couldn't afford to be distracted from Party Queens by heartbreak at such a crucial time in the growth of her business.

The set of his jaw made him seem very serious. 'I didn't want to waste your time when I had nothing to offer you. But ultimately I had to see you.'

'Six months later? Maybe you should have let *me* be the one to decide whether I wanted to waste my time or not?' She willed any hint of a wobble from her voice.

'I needed that time on my own. Possibly it was a mistake not to communicate that with you. I was married a long time. Now I'm single again at thirty-two. I haven't had a lot of practice at this.'

Eliza stared in disbelief at the gorgeous man beside her in the driver's seat. At his handsome profile with the slightly crooked nose and strong jaw. His shoulders so broad they took up more than his share of the car. His tanned arms, strong and muscular, dusted with hair that glinted gold in the sunlight coming through the window of the car. His hands— Best she did not think about those hands and how they'd felt on her bare skin back in magical Montovia.

'I find that difficult to buy,' she said. 'You're a really good-looking guy. There must be women stampeding to date you.'

He shrugged dismissively. 'All that eligible billionaire stuff the media likes to bang on about brings a certain level of attention. Even before the divorce was through I had women hounding me with dollar signs blazing in their eyes.'

'I guess that kind of attention comes with the territory. But surely not *everyone* would be a gold-digger. You must have dated *some* genuine women.'

She hated the thought of him with another woman. Not his ex-wife. That had been long before she'd met him. But Eliza had no claim on him—no right to be jealous. For all his fine talk about how he hadn't been able to forget her, the fact remained she was only here with him by accident.

Jake slowly shook his head. 'I haven't dated anyone since the divorce.' He paused for a long moment, the silence only broken by the swish of the tyres on the road, the air blowing from the air-conditioning unit.

Jake gave her another quick, sideward glance. 'Don't you get it, Eliza? There's only one woman who interests me. And she's sitting here, right beside me.'

Eliza suddenly understood the old expression about having all the wind blown out of her sails. A stunned, 'Oh...' was all she could manage through her suddenly accelerated breath.

Jake looked straight ahead as he spoke, as if he was finding the words difficult to get out. 'The support group covered dating after divorce. It suggested six months before starting to date. Three months was long enough. The urge to see you again became overwhelming. I didn't get where I am in the world by following the rules. All that dating-after-divorce advice flew out the window.'

Eliza frowned. 'How can you *say* that? You left our seeing each other again purely to chance. If we hadn't met at the airport—'

'I didn't leave anything to chance. After six months of radio silence I doubted you'd welcome a call from me. Any communication needed to be face to face. I flew down to Sydney to see you. Then met with Dominic to suss out how the land lay.'

'You *what*? Andie didn't say anything to me.'

'Because I asked Dominic not to tell her. He found out you were flying to Port Douglas this morning. I couldn't believe you were heading for a town where I had a house. Straight away I booked onto the same flight.'

Eliza took a few moments to absorb this revelation. 'That was very cloak and dagger. What would have happened if you hadn't found me at the airport?'

He shrugged those broad shoulders. 'I would have abducted you.' At her gasp he added, 'Just kidding. But I *would* have found a way for us to reconnect in Port Douglas. Even if I'd had to call every resort and hotel I would have tracked you down. I just had to see you, Eliza. To see if that attraction I'd felt was real.'

'I… I don't know what to say. Except I'm flattered.'

There was a long beat before he spoke. 'And pleased?'

The tinge of uncertainty to his voice surprised her. 'Very pleased.'

In fact her heart was doing cartwheels of exultation. She was so dizzy that the warning from her brain was having trouble getting through. Jake tracking her down sounded very romantic. So did his talk of abduction. But she'd learned to be wary of the type of man who would ride roughshod over her wishes and needs. Like her domineering father. Like her controlling ex. She didn't know Jake very well. It must take a certain kind of ruthlessness to become a billionaire. She couldn't let her guard down.

'So, about that coffee we talked about…?' he said. 'Do you want to make it lunch?'

'Are you asking me on a *date*, Jake?' Her tone was deliberately flirtatious.

His reply was very serious. 'I realise I've surprised you with this. But be assured I've released the baggage of my marriage. I've accepted my authentic self. And if you—'

She couldn't help a smile. 'You sound like you've swallowed the "dating after divorce" handbook.'

His brows rose. 'I told you I was out of practice. What else should I say?'

Eliza started to laugh. 'This is getting a little crazy.

Pull over, will you, please?' she said. She indicated a layby ahead with a wave of her hand.

Jake did so with a sudden swerve and squealing of tyres that had her clutching onto the dashboard of the car. He skidded to a halt under the shade of some palm trees.

Still laughing, Eliza unbuckled her seatbelt and turned to face him. 'Can I give you a dating after divorce tip? Don't worry so much about whether it's going to lead to something serious before you've even gone on a first date.'

'Was that what I did?'

She found his frown endearing. How could a guy who was one of the most successful entrepreneurs in the country be having this kind of trouble?

'You're over-thinking all this,' she said. 'So am I. We're making it so much harder than it should be. In truth, it's simple. There's an attraction here. You're divorced. I'm divorced. We don't answer to anyone except ourselves. There's nothing to stop us enjoying each other's company in any way we want to.'

He grinned in that lazy way she found so attractive. 'Nothing at all.'

'Shall we agree not to worry about tomorrow when we haven't even had a today yet?'

Eliza had been going to add *not even a morning*. But that conjured up an image of waking up next to Jake, in a twist of tangled sheets. Better not think about mornings. Or nights.

Jake's grin widened. 'You've got four days of vacation. I've got nothing to do except decide whether or not to offload my house in Port Douglas.'

'No expectations. No promises. No apologies.'

'Agreed,' he said. He held out his hand to shake and seal the deal.

She edged closer to him. 'Forget the handshake. Why don't we start with a kiss?'

CHAPTER FOUR

JAKE KNEW THERE was a dating after divorce guideline regarding the first physical encounter, but he'd be damned if he could think about that right now. Any thoughts other than of Eliza had been blown away in a blaze of anticipation and excitement at the invitation in her eyes—a heady mix of sensuality, impatience and mischief.

It seemed she had forgiven him for his broken promise. He had a second chance with her. It was so much more than he could have hoped for—or probably deserved after his neglect.

He hadn't told her the whole truth about why he hadn't been in touch. It was true he hadn't been able to forget her, had felt compelled to see her again. He was a man who liked to be in the company of one special woman and he'd hungered for her. But not necessarily to commit to anything serious. Not now. Maybe not ever again. Not with her. Not with any woman. However it seemed she wasn't looking for anything serious either. Four days without strings? That sounded like a great idea.

She slid a little closer to him from her side of the car. Reached down and unbuckled his seat belt with a low, sweet laugh that sent his awareness levels soaring. When her fingers inadvertently trailed over his thigh he shuddered and pulled her kissing distance close.

He focused with intense anticipation on her sweet mouth. Her lips were beautifully defined, yet lush and soft and welcoming. She tilted her face to him, making her impatience obvious. Jake needed no urging. He pressed his mouth against hers in a tender kiss, claiming her at last. She tasted of salt—peanuts on the plane, perhaps?—and something sweet. Chocolate? Sweet and sharp at the same time. Like Eliza herself—an intriguing combination.

She was beautiful, but his attraction had never been just to her looks. He liked her independence, her intelligence, her laughter.

The kiss felt both familiar and very different. Within seconds it was as if *her* kiss was all he'd ever known. Her lips parted under his as she gave a soft sigh of contentment.

'At last,' she murmured against his mouth.

Kissing Eliza for the first time in the front seat of a four-by-four was hardly ideal. Jake had forgotten how awkward it was to make out in a car. But having Eliza in his arms was way too exciting to be worrying about the discomfort of bumping into the steering wheel or handbrake. She held his face between her hands as she returned his kiss, her tongue sliding between his lips to meet his, teasing and exploring. He was oblivious to the car, their surroundings, the fact that they were parked in a public layby. He just wanted to keep kissing Eliza.

Was it seconds or minutes before Eliza broke away from him? That kind of excitement wasn't easily measured. Her cheeks were flushed, her eyes shades brighter, her lips swollen and pouting. She was panting, so it took her some effort to control her voice. 'Kissing you was all I could think about that night in the castle.'

'Me too,' he said.

Only his thoughts had marched much further than kissing. That last night he hadn't been able to sleep, taunted by the knowledge she was in the apartment next to his at the castle, overwhelmed by how much he wanted her. Back then his married state had been an obstacle. Now there was nothing stopping them from acting on the attraction between them.

He claimed her mouth again, deeper, more demanding. There'd been enough talking. He was seized with a sense of urgency to be with her while he could. He wasn't going to 'over-think' about where this might lead. Six months of pent-up longing for this woman erupted into passion, fierce and hungry.

As their kiss escalated in urgency Jake pulled her onto his lap, one hand around her waist, the other resting against the side of the car to support her. He bunched her hair in his hand and tugged to tilt her face upward, so he could deepen the kiss, hungry for her, aching for more. The little murmurs of pleasure she made deep in her throat drove him crazy with want.

His hands slid down her bare arms, brushed the side curves of her breasts, the silkiness of her top. She gasped, placed both hands on his chest and pushed away. She started to laugh—that delightful, chiming laughter he found so enchanting.

'We're steaming up the windows here like a coupled of hormone-crazed adolescents,' she said, her voice broken with laughter.

'What's wrong with being hormone-crazed *adults*,' he said, his own voice hoarse and unsteady.

'Making out in a car is seriously sexy. I don't want to stop,' she said, moaning when he nuzzled against the delicious softness of her throat, kissing and tasting.

The confined area of the car was filled with her scent, heady and intoxicating. 'Me neither,' he said.

Eliza was so relaxed and responsive she took away any thought of awkwardness. He glanced over to the back seat. There was more room there. It was wider and roomier.

'The back seat would be more comfortable,' he said.

He kissed her again, manoeuvring her towards the door. They would have to get out and transfer to the back, though it might be a laugh to try and clamber through the gap between the front seats. Why not?

Just then another car pulled into the layby and parked parallel to the four-by-four. Eliza froze in his arms. Their mouths were still pressed together. Her eyes communicated her alarm.

'That puts paid to the back seat plan,' he said, pulling away from her with a groan of regret.

'Just as well, really,' Eliza said breathlessly.

She smoothed her hair back from her face with her fingers and tucked it behind her ears. Even her ears were lovely—small and shell-like.

'The media would love to catch their most eligible bachelor being indiscreet in public.'

He scowled. 'I hate the way they call me a *bachelor*. Surely that's a term for someone who has never been married?'

'*Most eligible divorcé* doesn't quite have the same headline potential, does it?' she said.

'I'd rather not feature in *any* headlines,' he growled.

'You might just have to hit yourself with the ugly stick, then,' she said. 'Handsome and rich makes you a magnet for headlines. You're almost too good to be true.' She laughed. 'Though if you scowl like that they might forget about calling you the most eligible guy in the country.'

Jake exaggerated the scowl. He liked making her laugh. 'Too good to be true, huh?'

'Now you look cute,' she said.

'*Cute?* I do *not* want to be called cute,' he protested.

'Handsome, good-looking, hot, smokin', babelicious—'

'Stop right there,' he said, unable to suppress a grin. 'You don't call a guy *babelicious*. That's a girl word. Let me try it on you.'

'No need,' she protested. 'I'm not the babelicious type.'

'I think you are—if I understand it to mean sexy and desirable and—' Her mock glare made him stop. 'How about lovely, beautiful, sweet, elegant—?'

'That's more than enough,' she said. 'I'll take elegant. Audrey Hepburn's style is my icon. Not that I'm really tall enough to own *elegant*. But I try.'

'You succeed, let me assure you,' he said.

'Thank you. I like *smokin*' for you,' she said, her eyes narrowing as she looked him over.

Her flattering descriptive words left him with a warm feeling. No matter how he'd tried to put a brave face on it, the continued rejection by his ex had hurt. She'd found someone else, of course. He should have realised earlier, before he'd let his ego get so bruised.

The admiration in Eliza's eyes was like balm to those bruises. He intended to take everything she offered.

'I'd rather kiss than talk, wouldn't you?' he said.

He'd rather do so much more than kiss.

'If you say so,' she said with a seductive smile.

They kissed for a long time, until just kissing was not enough. It was getting steamy in the car—and not in an exciting way. It was too hot without the air-conditioning, but they couldn't sit there with the engine on.

The windows really were getting fogged up now. Visibility was practically zero. Eliza swiped her finger across the windscreen. Then spelled out the word KISSING. 'It's very obvious what's going on in here.'

He found her wicked giggle enchanting.

'More so now you've done that,' he said.

Spontaneity wasn't something he'd expected from cool and controlled Eliza. He ached to discover what other surprises she had in store for him.

'We really should go,' she said breathlessly. 'How long will it take to get to Port Douglas?'

'Thirty minutes to my place,' he said.

She wiggled in her seat in a show of impatience. 'Then put your foot to the floor and get us there ASAP, will you?'

Jake couldn't get his foot on the accelerator fast enough.

Eliza had a sense she was leaving everything that was everyday behind her as the four-by-four effortlessly climbed the steep driveway which led from the street in Port Douglas to Jake's getaway house. His retreat, he'd called it. As she slid out of the high-set car she gaped at the magnificence of the architectural award-winning house nestled among palm trees and vivid tropical gardens. Large glossy leaves in every shade of green contrasted with riotous blooms in orange, red and yellow. She breathed in air tinged with salt, ginger and the honey-scented white flowers that grew around the pathway.

This was his second house. No, his third. He'd told her he had a penthouse apartment in one of the most fashionable waterfront developments in Sydney, where his neighbours were celebrities and millionaires. His riverfront mansion in Brisbane was his home base. There were probably other houses too, but she'd realised early on that Jake wasn't the kind of billionaire to boast about his wealth.

Then Jake was kissing her again, and she didn't think about houses or bank balances or anything other than him and the way he was making her feel. He didn't break the kiss as he used his fingerprints on a sensor to get into the house—nothing so mundane as a key—and pushed open the door. They stumbled into the house, still kissing, laughing at their awkward progress but refusing to let go of each other.

Once inside, Eliza registered open-plan luxury and an awesome view. Usually she was a sucker for a water view. But nothing could distract her from Jake. She'd never wanted a man more than she wanted him. Many times since the wedding in Montovia she'd wondered if she had been foolish in holding off from him. There would be no regrets this time—no 'if only'. She didn't want him to stop…didn't want second thoughts to sneak into her consciousness.

In the privacy of the house their kisses got deeper, more demanding. Caresses—she of him and he of her—got progressively more intimate. Desire, warm and urgent, thrilled through her body.

She remembered when she'd first met Jake. He'd flown down to Sydney to be best man for Dominic at the surprise wedding Dominic had organised for Andie. Eliza had been expecting a geek. The athletic, handsome best man had been the furthest from her image of a geek as he could possibly have been. She'd been instantly smitten—then plunged into intense disappointment to find he was married.

Now she had the green light to touch him, kiss him, undress him. *No holds barred.*

'Bedroom?' he murmured.

He didn't really have to ask. There had been no need for words for her to come to her decision of where to take this mutually explosive passion. Their kisses, their caresses, their sighs had communicated everything he needed to know.

She had always enjoyed those scenes in movies where a kissing couple left a trail of discarded clothing behind them as they staggered together towards the bedroom. To be taking part in such a scene with Jake was like a fantasy fulfilled. A fantasy that had commenced in the ballroom of a fairytale castle in Europe and culminated in an ultra-modern house overlooking a tropical beach in far north Australia.

They reached his bedroom, the bed set in front of a panoramic view that stretched out over the pool to the sea. Then she was on the bed with Jake, rejoicing in the intimacy, the closeness, the confidence—the wonderful new entity that was *them*.

Eliza and Jake.

CHAPTER FIVE

ELIZA DIDN'T KNOW where she was when she woke up some time later. In a super-sized bed and not alone. She blinked against the late-afternoon sunlight streaming through floor-to-ceiling windows with a view of palm trees, impossibly blue sky, the turquoise sea beyond.

Jake's bedroom.

She smiled to herself with satisfaction. Remembered the trail of discarded clothes that had led to this bed. The passion. The fun. The ultimate pleasure. Again and again.

He lay beside her on his back, long muscular limbs sprawled across the bed and taking up much of the space. The sheets were tangled around his thighs. He seemed to be in a deep sleep, his broad chest rhythmically rising and falling.

She gazed at him for a long moment and caught her breath when she remembered what a skilled, passionate lover he'd proved to be. Her body ached in a thoroughly satisfied way.

Beautiful wasn't a word she would normally choose to describe a man. But he *was* beautiful—in an intensely masculine way. The tawny hair, green eyes—shut tight at the moment—the sculpted face, smooth tanned skin, slightly crooked nose. His beard had started to shadow his jaw, dark in contrast to the tawny blond of his hair.

There were some things in life she would never, ever forget or regret. Making love with Jake was one of them. Heaven knew where they went from here, but even if this was all she ever had of him she would cherish the memory for the rest of her days. In her experience it was rare to want someone so intensely and then not be disappointed. Nothing about making love with Jake disappointed her.

Eliza breathed in the spicy warm scent of him; her own classic French scent that was her personal indulgence mingled with it so that it became the scent of *them*. Unique, memorable, intensely personal.

She tentatively stretched out a leg. It was starting to cramp under his much larger, heavier leg. Rolling cautiously away, so her back faced him, she wondered where the bathroom was, realised it was en suite and so not far.

She started to edge cautiously away. Then felt a kiss on her shoulder. She went still, her head thrown back in pleasure as Jake planted a series of kisses along her shoulder to land a final one in her most sensitive spot at the top of her jaw, below her ear. She gasped. They had so quickly learned what pleased each other.

Then a strong arm was around her, restraining her. 'You're not going anywhere,' he said as he pulled her to him.

She turned around to find Jake lying on his side. His body was so perfect she gasped her admiration. The sculptured pecs, the flat belly and defined six-pack, the muscular arms and legs... He was without a doubt the hottest billionaire on the planet.

Eliza trailed her hand over the smooth skin of his chest. *'Smokin','* she murmured.

He propped himself up on his other elbow. Smiled that slow smile. 'Okay?' he asked.

'Very okay,' she said, returning his smile and stretching like one of her cats with remembered pleasure. 'It was very sudden. Unexpected. So soon, I mean. But it was good we just let it happen. We didn't get a chance to over-think things. Over-analyse how we felt, what it would mean.'

'Something so spontaneous wasn't in my dating after divorce guidebook,' he said with that endearing grin.

His face was handsome, but strong-jawed and tough. That smile lightened it, took away the edge of ruthlessness she sensed was not far from the surface. He couldn't have got where he had by being Mr Nice Guy. That edge excited her.

'Lucky you threw it out the window, then,' she said. 'I seriously wonder about the advice in that thing.'

'Best thing I ever did was ignore it,' he said.

He kissed her lightly on the shoulder, the growth of his beard pleasantly rough. She felt a rush of intense triumph that she was here with him—finally. With her finger she traced around his face, exploring its contours, the feel of his skin, smooth in parts, rough with bristle in others. Yes, she could call this man *beautiful.*

He picked up a strand of her hair and idly twisted it between his fingers. 'What did you do to get over *your* divorce?'

The question surprised her. It wasn't something she

really wanted to remember. 'Became a hermit for a while. Like you, I felt an incredible sense of failure. I'm not used to failing at things. There was relief though, too. We got married when I was twenty-four. I'd only known him six months when he marched me down the aisle. Not actually an aisle. He'd been married before so we got hitched in the registry office.'

'Why the hurry?'

'He was seven years older than me. He wanted to start a family. I should have known better than to be rushed into it. Big mistake. Turned out I didn't know him at all. He showed himself to be quite the bully.'

She had ended up both fearing and hating him.

'Sounds like you had a lucky escape.'

'I did. But it wasn't pleasant at the time. No break-up ever is, is it? No matter the circumstances.'

Jake nodded assent. 'Mine dragged on too long.'

'I know. I was waiting, remember.'

'It got so delayed at the end because her new guy inserted himself into the picture. He introduced an element of ugliness and greed.'

Ugliness. Eliza didn't want to admit to Jake how scary *her* marriage had become. There hadn't been physical abuse, but she had endured some serious mental abuse. When she'd found herself getting used to it, even making excuses for Craig because she'd hated to admit she'd made a mistake in marrying him, she'd known it was time to get out. The experience had wounded her and toughened her. She'd vowed never again to risk getting tied up in something as difficult to extricate herself from as marriage.

'It took me a while to date again,' she said. 'I'd lost faith in my judgement of men. Man, did I date a few duds. And I turned off a few guys who were probably quite decent because of my interrogation technique. I found myself trying to discover anything potentially wrong about them before I even agreed to go out for a drink.'

Jake used her hair to tug her gently towards him for a quick kiss on her nose before he released her. 'You didn't interrogate me,' he said.

'I didn't need to. You weren't a potential date. When we first met at Andie and Dominic's wedding you were married. I could chat to you without expectation or agenda. You were an attractive, interesting man but off-limits.'

He picked up her hand, began idly stroking first her palm and then her fingers. Tingles of pleasure shot through her body right down to her toes. Nothing was off-limits now.

'You were so lovely, so smart—and so accepting of me,' he said. 'It was a revelation. You actually seemed interested in what I had to say.'

As his ex hadn't been? Eliza began to see how unhappy Jake had been. Trapped in a past-its-use-by-date marriage. Bound by what seemed to have been misplaced duty and honour.

'Are you kidding me?' she said. 'You're such a success story and only a few years older than me. I found you fascinating. And a surprise. All three Party Queens had been expecting a stereotype geek—not a guy who looked like an athlete. You weren't arrogant either, which was another surprise.'

'That was a social situation. I can be arrogant when it comes to my work and impatient with people who don't get it.'

His expression hardened and she saw again that underlying toughness. She imagined he would be a demanding boss.

'I guess you have to be tough to have got where you are—a self-made man. Your fortune wasn't handed to you.'

'I see you've done your research?'

'Of course.' She'd spent hours on the internet, looking him up—not that'd she'd admit to the extent of her 'research'. 'There's a lot to be found on Jake Marlowe. The media loves a rags-to-riches story.'

'There were never rags. Clothes from charity shops, yes, but not rags.' The tense lines of his mouth belied his attempt at a joke. 'My mother did her best to make life as good for me as she could. But it wasn't easy. Struggle Street is not where I ever wanted to stay. Or go back to. My ex never really got that.'

'You married young. Why?' There hadn't been a lot in the online information about his early years.

He replied without hesitation. 'Fern was pregnant. It was the right thing to do.'

'I thought you didn't have kids?'

'I don't. She lost the baby quite early.'

'That's sad…' Her voice trailed away. *Very* sad. She would not—could not—reveal how very sad the thought made her. How her heart shrank a little every time she thought about having kids.

'The pregnancy was an accident.'

'Not a ploy to force your hand in marriage?' She had always found the 'oldest trick in the book' to be despicable.

'No. We'd been together off and on since my last year of high school. Marriage was the next step. The pregnancy just hurried things along. Looking back on it, though, I can see if she hadn't got pregnant we might not have ended up married. It was right on the cusp, when everything was changing. Things were starting to take off in a big way for the company Dominic and I had started.'

'You didn't try for a baby again?'

'Fern didn't want kids. Felt the planet was already over-populated. That it was irresponsible to have children.'

'And you?' She held her breath for his answer.

During her infrequent forays into dating she'd found the children issue became urgent for thirty-somethings. For women there was the very real fact of declining fertility. And men like her ex thought they had biological clocks too. Craig had worried about being an old dad. He'd been obsessed with being able to play active sports with his kids. Boys, of course, in particular. Having come from a farming family, where boys had been valued more than girls, that had always rankled with her.

Jake's jaw had set and she could see the hard-headed businessman under the charming exterior.

'I've never wanted to have children. My ex and I were in agreement about not wanting kids.'

'What about in the future?'

He shook his head. 'I won't change my mind. I don't want to be a father. *Ever*.'

'I see,' she said, absorbing what he meant. What it meant to her. It was something she didn't want to share with him at this stage. She might be out of here this afternoon and never see him again.

'My support group devoted a lot of time to warnings

about women who might try and trap a wealthy, newly single guy into marriage by getting pregnant,' he said.

'Doesn't it take two to get a woman pregnant?'

'The odds can be unfairly stacked when one half of the equation lies about using contraception.'

Eliza pulled a face. 'Those poor old gold-diggers again. I don't know *any* woman I could label as a gold-digger, and we do parties through all echelons of Sydney society. Are there really legions of women ready to trap men into marriage by getting pregnant?'

'I don't know about legions, but they definitely exist. The other guys in that group were proof of that. It can be a real problem for rich men. A baby means lifetime child support—that's a guaranteed income for a certain type of woman.'

'But surely—'

Jake put up a hand at her protest. 'Hear me out. Some of those men were targeted when they were most vulnerable. It's good to be forewarned. I certainly wouldn't want to find myself caught in a trap like that.'

'Well, you don't have to worry about me,' she said. In light of this conversation, she *had* to tell him. 'I can't—'

He put a finger over her mouth. She took it between her teeth and gently nipped it.

'Be assured I don't think of you like that,' he said. 'Your fierce independence is one of the things I like about you.'

'Seriously, Jake. Listen to me. I wouldn't be able to hold you to ransom with a pregnancy because…because…' How she hated admitting to her failure to be able to fulfil a woman's deepest biological purpose. 'I… I can't have children.'

He stilled. 'Eliza, I'm sorry. I didn't know.'

'Of course you didn't know. It's not something I blurt out too often.' She hated to be defined by her infertility. Hated to be pitied. *Poor Eliza—you know she can't have kids?*

'How? Why?'

'I had a ruptured appendix when I was twelve years old. No one took it too seriously at first. They put my tummy pains down to something I ate. Or puberty. But the pain got worse. By the time they got me to hospital—remember we lived a long way from the nearest town—the appendix had burst and septicaemia had set in.'

Jake took her hand, gripped it tight. 'Eliza, I'm so sorry. Couldn't the doctors have done something?'

'I don't know. I was twelve and very ill. Turned out I was lucky to be alive. Unfortunately no one told me, or my parents, what damage it had done to my reproductive system—the potential for scar tissue on the fallopian tubes. I wasn't aware of the problem until I tried to have a baby and couldn't fall pregnant. Only then was I told that infertility is a not uncommon side effect of a burst appendix.'

He frowned. 'I really don't know what to say.'

'What *can* you say? Don't try. You can see why I don't like to talk about it.'

'You said your ex wanted to start a family? Is that why you split?'

'In part, yes. He was already over thirty and he really wanted to have kids. His *own* kids. Adoption wasn't an option for him. I wanted children too, though probably later rather than sooner. I never thought I wouldn't be able to have a baby. I always believed I would be a mother. And one day a grandmother. Even a great-grandmother. I'll miss out on all of that.'

'I'm sorry, Eliza,' he said again.

She couldn't admit to him—to anyone—her deep, underlying sense of failure as a woman. How she grieved the loss of her dream of being a mother, which had died when the truth of her infertility had been forced into her face with the results of scans and X-rays.

'They don't test you until after a year of unsuccessfully trying to get pregnant,' she said. 'Then the tests take a while. My ex couldn't deal with it. By that stage he thought he'd invested enough time in me.'

Jake spat out a number of choice names for her ex. Eliza didn't contradict him.

'By that stage he'd proved what a dreadful, controlling man he was and I was glad to be rid of him. Still, my sense of failure was multiplied by his reaction. He actually used the word "barren" at one stage. How old-fashioned was that?'

'I'd call it worse than that. I'd call it cruel.'

'I guess it was.' One of a long list of casual cruelties he'd inflicted on her.

Eliza hadn't wanted to introduce such a heavy subject into her time with Jake, those memories were best left buried.

'Where did you meet this jerk—your ex, I mean—and not know what he was really like? Online?'

'At work. I told you when I first met you how I started my working life as an accountant at a magazine publishing company. I loved the industry, and jumped at the chance to move into the sales side when it came up. My success there and my finance background gave me a good shot at a publisher's role with another company. He was my boss at the new company.'

'You married the boss?'

'The classic cliché,' she said. 'But what made him a good publisher made him a terrible husband. Now, I don't want to waste another second talking about him. He's in my past and staying there. I moved to a different publishing company—and a promotion—and never looked back. Then when the next magazine I worked on folded—as happens in publishing—Andie, Gemma and I started Party Queens.'

'And became the most in-demand party-planners in Sydney,' he said.

Sometimes it seemed to Eliza as if her brief marriage had never happened. But the wounds Craig had left behind him were still there. She'd been devastated at the doctor's prognosis of infertility caused by damaged fallopian tubes. Craig had only thought about what it meant to *him*. Eliza had realised she couldn't live with his mental abuse. But she still struggled with doubt and distrust when it came to men.

Thank heaven she'd had the sense to insist they signed a pre-nup. He'd had no claim on her pre-marriage apartment, and she'd emerged from the marriage financially unscathed.

'I suppose your "dating after divorce" advice included getting a watertight pre-nup before any future nuptials?' she said. 'I'm here to suggest it's a good idea. To add to all his faults, my ex proved to be an appalling money-manager.'

'Absolutely,' he said. 'That was all tied up with the gold-digger advice.'

Eliza laughed, but she was aware of a bitter edge to

her laughter. 'I interrogated all my potential dates to try and gauge if they were controlling bullies like my ex. You're on the lookout for gold-diggers. Are we too wounded by our past experiences just to accept people for what they appear to be?'

Jake's laugh added some welcome levity to the conversation. 'You mean the way you and I have done?' he said.

Eliza thought about that for a long moment. Of course. That was exactly what they'd done. They'd met with no expectation or anticipation.

'Good point,' she conceded with an answering smile. 'We just discovered we liked each other, didn't we? In the old-fashioned boy-meets-girl way. The best man and the bridesmaid.'

'But then had to wait it out until we could pursue the attraction,' he said.

She reached out and placed her hand on his cheek, reassuring herself that he really was there and not one of the dreams she'd had of him after she'd got home from Montovia. 'And here we are.'

When it came to a man, Eliza had never shut down her good sense to this extent. She wasn't looking any further ahead than right here, right now. She'd put caution on the back burner and let her libido rule and she intended to enjoy the unexpected gift of time with this man she'd wanted since she'd first met him.

Jake went to pull her closer. Mmm, they could start all over again... Just then her stomach gave a loud, embarrassing rumble. Eliza wished she could crawl under the sheets and disappear.

But Jake smiled. 'I hear you. My stomach's crying out the same way. It's long past lunchtime.'

As he got up from the bed the sheet fell from him. Naked, he walked around the room with a complete lack of inhibition. He was magnificent. Broad shoulders tapered down to a muscled back and the most perfect male butt, his skin there a few shades lighter than his tan elsewhere. He was just gorgeous. The prototype specimen of the human male. She felt a moment's regret for humanity that his genes weren't going to be passed on to a new generation. That combination of awesome body and amazing brain wouldn't happen too often.

She had nothing to be ashamed of about her own body—she worked out and kept fit. But she suddenly felt self-conscious about being naked and tugged the sheets up over her chest. It was only this morning that she'd encountered him at the airport lounge. She wasn't a one-night stand kind of person. Or hadn't been up until now. *Until Jake.*

He slung on a pale linen robe. 'I'll go check what food there is in the kitchen while you get dressed.'

Eliza remembered their frantic dash into the bedroom a few hours before. 'My bag with my stuff in it—it's still in the car.'

'It's in the dressing room,' said Jake, pointing in the direction of the enormous walk-in closet. 'I went out to the car after you fell asleep. Out like a light and snoring within seconds.'

Eliza gasped. 'I do *not* snore!' *Did* she? It was so long since she'd shared a bed with someone she wouldn't know.

'Heavy breathing, then,' Jake teased. 'Anyway, I brought your bag in and put it in there.'

'Thank you,' said Eliza.

The bathroom was as luxurious as the rest of the house. All natural marble and bold, simple fittings like in an upscale hotel. She quickly showered. Then changed into a vintage-inspired white sundress with a full skirt and wedge-heeled white sandals she'd bought just for the vacation.

Standing in front of the mirror, she ran a brush through the tangles of her hair. Then scrutinised her face to wipe the smeared mascara from under her eyes. Thank heavens for waterproof—it hadn't developed into panda eyes. She slicked on a glossy pink lipstick.

Until now she hadn't planned on wearing make-up at all this vacation. But hooking up with Jake had changed all that. Suddenly she felt the need to look her most feminine best. She wanted more than a one-night stand. Four days stretched out ahead of her in Port Douglas and she hoped she'd spend all of them with Jake. After that—who knew?

CHAPTER SIX

JAKE WAITED IMPATIENTLY for Eliza to get dressed and join him in the living area. He couldn't believe she was here in his house with him. It was more than he could have hoped for when he'd intercepted her at the airport.

He welcomed the everyday sounds of running taps, closing doors, footsteps tapping on the polished concrete floors. Already Eliza's laughter and her sweet scent had transformed the atmosphere. He'd like to leave that sexy trail of clothing down the hallway in place as a permanent installation.

This house was a prize in a property portfolio that was filled with magnificent houses. But it seemed he had always been alone and unhappy here. There had been many opportunities for infidelity during the waning months of his marriage but he'd never taken them up. He'd always thought of himself as a one-woman man.

That mindset had made him miserable while he'd refused to accept the demise of his marriage. But meeting Eliza, a woman as utterly different from his ex as it was possible to be, had shown him a different possible path. However he hadn't been ready to set foot on that path. Not so soon after the tumult and turmoil that had driven him off the rails to such detriment to his business.

Extricating himself from a marriage gone bad had made him very wary about risking serious involvement again. He'd stayed away from Eliza for that very reason—she did not appear to be a pick-her-up-and-put-her-down kind of woman, and he didn't want to hurt her. Or have his own heart broken. Ultimately, however, he'd been *compelled* to see her again—despite the advice from his divorce support group and his own hard-headed sense of self-preservation.

She'd told him he'd been over-thinking the situation. Too concerned about what *might* happen before they'd even started anything. Then she'd gifted him with this no-strings interlude. *No expectations or promises, no apologies if it didn't work out.* What more could a man ask for?

Eliza had surprised and enthralled him with her warm sensuality and lack of inhibition. He intended to make the most of her four days in Port Douglas. Starting by ensuring that she spent the entire time of her vacation with him.

He sensed Eliza's tentative entry into the room from the kitchen before he even heard her footsteps. He looked up and his breath caught at the sight of her in a white dress that was tight at her waist and then flared to show off her slim figure and shapely legs.

He gave a wolf whistle of appreciation. 'You're looking very babelicious.'

Her eyes narrowed in sensual appraisal as she slowly looked him up and down. 'You don't look too smokin' bad yourself,' she said.

He'd quickly gone into one of the other bathrooms, showered and changed into shorts and a T-shirt.

'Comfortable is my motto,' he said. He dragged at his neck as if at an imaginary necktie. 'I hate getting trussed up in a suit and tie.'

'I don't blame you. I feel sorry for guys in suits, sweltering in the heat of an Australian summer.'

'It's a suit-free zone at *my* company headquarters.' A tech company didn't need to keep corporate dress rules.

'I enjoy fashion,' she said. 'After a childhood spent in jeans and riding boots—mostly hand-me-downs from my brothers—I can't get enough girly clothes.'

'Your dress looks like something from my grandma's wardrobe,' he said. Then slammed his hand against his forehead 'That didn't come out quite as I meant it to. I meant from when my grandma was young.'

'You mean it has a nice vintage vibe?' she said. 'I take that as a compliment. I love retro-inspired fashion.'

'It suits you,' he said. He thought about saying that he preferred her in nothing at all. Decided it was too soon.

She looked around her. 'So this is your vacation house? It's amazing.'

'Not bad, is it?'

The large open-plan rooms, with soaring ceilings, contemporary designer furniture, bold artworks by local artists, were all designed to showcase the view and keep the house cool in the tropical heat of far north Queensland. As well as to withstand the cyclones that lashed at this area of the coast with frequent violence.

'He says, with the modest understatement of a billionaire…' she said.

Jake liked her attitude towards his wealth. He got irritated by people who treated him with awe because of it. Very few people knew the truth about his past. How closely he'd courted disaster. But a mythology had built up around him and Dominic—two boys from nowhere who had burst unheralded into the business world.

He had worked hard, but he acknowledged there had been a certain element of luck to his meteoric success. People referred to him as a genius, but there were other people as smart as he—smarter, even—who could have identified the same need for ground-breaking software. He'd been in the right place at the right time and had been savvy enough to recognise it and act on it—to his and Dominic's advantage. Then he'd had the smarts to employ skilled programmers to get it right. Come to think of it, maybe there *was* a certain genius to that. Especially as he had replicated his early success over and over again.

'I found some gourmet pizzas in the freezer,' he said. 'I shoved a couple of them in the oven. There's salad too.'

'I wondered what smelled so good,' she said. 'Breakfast seems a long time ago.'

'We can eat out for dinner. There are some excellent restaurants in Port Douglas—as you no doubt know.'

'Yes…' she said. Her brow pleated into a frown. 'But I need to check in at my resort. I haven't even called them. They might give my room to someone else.'

'Wouldn't you rather stay here?' he asked.

Her eyes narrowed. 'Is that a trick question?'

'No tricks,' he said. 'It's taken us a long time—

years—to get the chance to spend time together. Why waste more time to-ing and fro-ing from a resort to here? This is more private. This is—'

'This is fabulous. Better than any resort. Of course I'd like to stay here. But is it too soon to be—?'

'Over-thinking this?'

'You're throwing my own words right back at me,' she said, with her delightful curving smile.

Her eyes seemed to reflect the colour of the sea in the vista visible through the floor-to-ceiling windows that looked out over the beach to the far reaches of the Pacific Ocean. He didn't think he'd ever met anyone with eyes of such an extraordinary blue. Eyes that showed what she was feeling. Right now he saw wariness and uncertainty.

'I would very much like to have you here with me,' he said. 'But of course it's entirely your choice. If you'd rather be at your resort I can drive you there whenever you want.'

'No! I… I want to be with you.'

'Good,' he said, trying to keep his cool and not show how gratified he was that he would have her all to himself. 'Then stay.'

'There's just one thing,' she said hesitantly. 'I feel a little…uncomfortable about staying here in a house you shared with your ex-wife. I notice there aren't any feminine touches in the bathroom and dressing room. But I—'

'She's never visited here,' he said. 'I bought this house as my escape when things started to get untenable in my marriage. That was not long before I met you at Dominic's wedding.'

'Oh,' she said.

'Does that make you feel better?' he asked.

She nodded. 'Lots better.'

He stepped closer, placed his hands on her shoulders, looked into her eyes. 'You're the only woman who has stayed here. Apart from my mother, who doesn't count as a woman.'

'I'm sure she'd be delighted to know that,' Eliza said, strangling a laugh.

'You know what I mean.' Jake felt more at home with numbers and concepts than words. Especially words evoking emotion and tension.

'Yes. I do. And I'm honoured to be the first.'

He took her in his arms for a long, sweet kiss.

The oven alarm went off with a raucous screech. They jumped apart. Laughed at how nervous they'd seemed.

'Lunch is ready,' he said. He was hungry, but he was tempted to ignore the food and keep on kissing Eliza. Different hungers required prioritising.

But Eliza had taken a step back from him. 'After we eat I need to cancel my resort booking,' she said. 'I'll have to pay for today, of course, but hopefully it will be okay for the other days. Not that I care, really. After all I—'

'I'll pay for any expense the cancellation incurs.'

He knew straight away from her change of expression that he'd made a mistake.

'You will *not* pay anything,' she said. 'That's my responsibility.'

Jake backed down straight away, put up his hands as if fending off attack. That was one argument he had no intention of pursuing. He would make it up to her in other ways—make sure she didn't need to spend another cent during her stay. He would organise everything.

'Right. I understand. My credit cards will remain firmly in my wallet unless you give me permission to wield them.'

She pulled a rueful face. 'Sorry if I overreacted. My independence is very important to me. I get a bit prickly when it's threatened. I run my own business and my own life. That's how I like it. And I don't want to ever have to answer to anyone again—for money or anything else.'

'Because of your ex-husband? You described him as controlling.'

'To be honest, he's turned me off the entire concept of marriage. And before him I had a domineering father who thought he had the right to rule my life even after I grew up.'

Jake placed his hand on her arm. 'Hold it right there. Don't take offence—I want to hear more. But right now I need food.' His snack on the plane seemed a long time ago.

She laughed. 'I grew up with three brothers. I know the rules. Number one being never to stand between a hungry man and his lunch.'

Jake grinned his relief at her reply. 'You're right. The pizza will burn, and I'm too hungry to wait to heat up more.'

'There are *more*?'

'The housekeeper has stocked the freezer with my favourite foods. She doesn't live in. I like my privacy too much for that. But she shops for me as well as keeps the house in order.'

'Unlimited pizza? Sounds good to me.'

From the look of her slim body, her toned muscles, he doubted Eliza indulged in pizza too often. But at his height and activity level he needed to eat a lot. There had been times when he was a kid he'd been hungry. Usually the day before his mother's payday, when she'd stretched their food as far as it would go. That would never happen again.

He headed for the oven. 'Over lunch I want to hear about that country upbringing of yours,' he said. 'I grew up here in Queensland, down on the Gold Coast. Inland Australia has always interested me.'

'Trust me, it was *not* idyllic. Farming is tough, hard work. A business like any other. Only with more variables out of the farmer's control.'

She followed him through the kitchen to the dining area, again with a view of the sea. 'I was about to offer to set the table,' she said. 'But I see you've beaten me to it.'

'I'm domesticated. My mother made sure of that. A single mum working long hours to keep a roof over our heads couldn't afford to have me pulling less than my weight,' he said.

That was when he'd chosen to *be* at home, of course. For a moment Jake wondered what Eliza would think of him if he revealed the whole story of his youth. She seemed so moralistic, he wondered if she could handle the truth about him. Not that he had any intention of telling her. There was nothing he'd told her already that couldn't be dug up on an online search—and she'd already admitted to such a search. The single mum. The hard times. His rise to riches in spite of a tough start. The untold story was in a sealed file never to be opened.

'It must have been tough for her. Your mother, I mean.'

'It was,' he said shortly. 'One of the good things about having money is that I can make sure she never has to worry again.' As a teenager he'd been the cause of most of her worries. As an adult he tried to make it up to her.

'So your mother lets you take care of her?'

'I don't give her much of a choice. I owe her so much and I will do everything I can to repay her. I convinced her to let me buy her a house and a business.'

'What kind of business did you buy for her?'

Of course Eliza would be interested in that. She was a hard-headed businesswoman herself.

'She worked as a waitress for years. Always wanted her own restaurant—thought she could do it better. Her café in one of the most fashionable parts of Brisbane is doing very well.' Again, this was nothing an online search wouldn't be able to find.

'There's obviously a family instinct for business,' she said.

He noted she didn't ask about his father, and he didn't volunteer the information.

'There could be something in that,' he said. 'She's on vacation in Tuscany at the moment—doing a residential Italian cooking course and having a ball.'

Eliza smiled. 'Not just a vacation. Sounds like it's work as well.'

'Isn't that the best type of work? Where the line between work and interest isn't drawn too rigidly?'

'Absolutely,' she said. 'I always enjoyed my jobs in publishing. But Party Queens is my passion. I couldn't imagine doing anything else now.'

'From what I hear Party Queens is so successful you never will.'

'Fingers crossed,' she said. 'I never take anything for granted, and I have to be constantly vigilant that we don't slip down from our success.'

She seated herself at the table, facing the view. He swooped the pizza onto the table with an exaggerated flourish, like he'd seen one of his mother's waiters do. 'Lunch is served, *signorina,*' he said.

Eliza laughed. 'You're quite the professional.'

'A professional heater-upper of pizza?'

'It isn't burned, and the cheese is all bubbly and perfect. You can take credit for *that.*'

Jake sat down opposite her. He wolfed down three large slices of pizza in the time it took Eliza to eat one. 'Now, tell me about life on the sheep ranch,' he said. And was surprised when her face stilled and all laughter fled from her expression.

Eliza sighed as she looked across the table at Jake. Her appetite for pizza had suddenly deserted her. 'Are you sure you want to hear about that?'

Did she want to relive it all for a man who might turn out to be just a fling? He'd told her something of the childhood that must have shaped the fascinating man he had become. But it was nothing she didn't already know. She really didn't like revisiting *her* childhood and adolescence. Not that it had been abusive, or anything near it. But she had been desperately unhappy and had escaped from home as soon as she could.

'Yes,' he said. 'I want to know more about you, Eliza.'

His gaze was intense on her face. She didn't know

him well enough to know what was genuine interest and what was part of a cultivated image of charm.

'Can I give you the short, sharp, abbreviated version?' she said.

'Go ahead,' he said, obviously bemused.

She took a deep, steadying breath. 'How about city girl at heart is trapped in a rural backwater where boys are valued more than girls?'

'It's a start.'

'You want more?'

He nodded.

'Okay...smart girl with ambition has hopes ridiculed.'

'Getting there,' he said. 'What's next?'

'Smart girl escapes to city and family never forgives her.'

'Why was that?' He frowned.

She knew there was danger now—of her voice getting wobbly. 'No easy answer. How about massive years-long drought ruins everything?' She took in another deep breath. 'It's actually difficult to make light of such disaster.'

'I can see that,' he said.

She wished he'd say there was no need to go on, but he didn't.

'Have you ever seen those images of previously lush green pastures baked brown and hard and cracked? Where farmers have to shoot their stock because there's no water, no feed? Shoot sheep that have not only been bred on your land so you care about their welfare, but also represent income and investment and your family's daily existence?'

'Yes. I've seen the pictures. Read the stories. It's terrible.'

'That was my family's story. Thankfully my father didn't lose his land or his life, like others did, before the rains eventually came. But he changed. Became harsher. Less forgiving. Impossible to live with. He took it out on my mother. And nothing *I* could do was right.'

Jake's head was tilted in what seemed like real interest. 'In what way?'

'Even at the best of times life in the country tends to be more traditional. Men are outdoors, doing the hard yakka—do you have that expression for hard work in Queensland?'

'Of course,' he said.

'Men are outside and women inside, doing the household chores to support the men. In physical terms it makes a lot of sense. And a lot of country folk like it just the way it's always been.'

'But you didn't?'

'No. School was where I excelled—maths and legal studies were my forte. My domestic skills weren't highly developed. I just wasn't that interested. And I wasn't great at farm work either, though I tried.' She flexed her right arm so her bicep showed, defined and firm. 'I'm strong, but not anywhere near as strong as my brothers. In my father's eyes I was useless. He wouldn't even let me help with the accounts; that was not my business. In a time of drought I was another mouth to feed and I didn't pull my weight.'

She could see she'd shocked Jake.

'Surely your father wouldn't really have thought that?' he said.

She remembered he'd grown up without a father.

'I wanted to be a lawyer. My father thought lawyers were a waste of space. My education was a drain on the farm. Looking back, I can see now how desperate he must have been. If he'd tried to communicate with me I might have understood. But he just walked all over me—as usual.'

'Seems like I've got you to open a can of worms. I'm sorry.'

She shrugged. 'You might as well hear the end of it. I was at boarding school. One day when I was seventeen I was called to the principal's office to find my father there to take me home so I could help my mother. For good. It was my final year of high school. I wasn't to be allowed to sit my end-of-school exams.'

Jake frowned. 'You're right—your dad must have been desperate. If there was no money to feed stock, school fees would have been out of the question.'

'For *me*. Not for my younger brother. My father found the fees for *him*.' She couldn't keep the bitterness from her voice. 'A boy who was never happier than when he was goofing off.'

'So the country girl went home? Is that how the story ended?'

She shook her head. 'Thankfully, no. I was a straight-A student—the school captain.'

'Why does that not surprise me?' said Jake wryly.

'The school got behind me. There was a scholarship fund. My family were able to plead hardship. I got to sit my final exams.'

'And blitzed them, no doubt?'

'Top of the state in three out of five subjects.'

'Your father must have been proud of you then.'

'If he was, he never said so. I'd humiliated him with the scholarship, and by refusing to go home with him.'

'Hardly a humiliation. Half of the eastern states were in one of the most severe droughts in Australia's history. Even *I* knew that at the time.'

'Try telling *him* that. He'd call it pride. I'd call it pig-headed stubbornness. The only thing that brought me and my father together was horses. We both loved them. I was on my first horse before I was two years old. The day our horses had to go was pretty well the end of any real communication between me and my father.'

There was real sympathy in his green eyes. 'You didn't have to shoot—?'

'We were lucky. A wonderful horse rescue charity took them to a different part of the state that wasn't suffering as much. The loss hit my father really hard.'

'And you too?'

She bowed her head. 'Yes.'

Jake was quiet for a long moment before he spoke again. 'You don't have to talk about this any more if you don't want to. I didn't realise how painful it would be for you.'

'S'okay,' she said. 'I might as well gallop to the finish.' She picked up her fork, put it down again, twisted a paper serviette between her fingers. 'Country girl wins scholarship to university in Sydney to study business degree. Leaves home, abandoning mother to her menfolk and a miserable marriage. No one happy about it but country girl…' Her voice trailed away.

Jake got up from the table and came to her side. He leaned down from behind her and wrapped big, strong muscular arms around her. 'Country girl makes good in the big city. That's a happy ending to the story.'

'I guess it is,' she said, leaning back against him, enjoying his strength and warmth, appreciating the way he was comforting her. 'My life now is just the way I want it.'

Except she couldn't have a baby. Underpinning it all was the one area of her life she'd been unable to control, where the body she kept so healthy and strong had let her down so badly.

She twisted around to look up at him. 'And Day One of my vacation is going perfectly.'

'So how about Days Two, Three and Four?' he said. 'If you were by yourself at your resort what would you be doing?'

'Relaxing. Lying by the pool.'

'We can do that here.'

'Swimming?'

'The pool awaits,' he said, gesturing to the amazing wet-edge pool outside the window, its aquamarine water glistening in the afternoon sunlight.

'That water is calling to me,' she said, twisting herself up and out of the chair so she stood in the circle of his arms, looking up at him. She splayed her hands against his chest, still revelling in the fact she could touch him.

For these few days he was hers.

His eyes narrowed. 'I'm just getting to know you, Eliza. But I suspect there's a list you want to check off before you fly home—you might even have scheduled some activities in to your days.'

'List? Schedules?' she said, pretending to look

around her. 'Have you been talking to Andie? She always teases me about the way I order my day.'

'I'm not admitting to anything,' he said. 'So there *is* a list?'

'We-e-ell...' She drew out the word. 'There *are* a few things I'd like to do. But only if you want to do them as well.'

'Fire away,' he said.

'One: go snorkelling on the Great Barrier Reef. Two: play golf on one of the fabulous courses up here. Then—'

Jake put up one large, well-shaped hand in a halt sign. 'Just wait there. Did I hear you say "play golf"?'

'Uh, yes. But you don't have to, of course. I enjoy golf. When I was in magazine advertising sales it was a very useful game to play. I signed a number of lucrative deals after a round with senior decision-makers.'

He lifted her up and swooped her around the room. 'Golf! The girl plays *golf.* One of my favourite sports.'

'You being a senior decision-maker and all,' she said with a smile.

'Me being a guy who likes to swing a club and slam a little white ball,' he said.

'In my case a neon pink ball. I can see it better on the fairway,' she said.

'She plays with a pink ball? Of *course* she does. Are you the perfect woman, Eliza Dunne?' He sounded more amused than mocking. 'I like snorkelling and diving too. Port Douglas is the right place to come for that. All can be arranged. Do you want to start checking off your list with a swim?'

'You bet.'

He looked deep into her face. Eliza thrilled to the message in his green eyes.

'The pool is very private. Swimsuits are optional.'

Eliza smiled—a long, slow smile of anticipation. 'Sounds very good to me.'

CHAPTER SEVEN

ELIZA SOON REALISED that a vacation in the company of a billionaire was very different from the vacation she had planned to spend on her own. Her own schedule of playing tourist and enjoying some quiet treatments in her resort spa had completely gone by the board.

That was okay, but she hadn't had any time to plan her strategy to keep the company thriving without the hands-on involvement of Gemma, Crown Princess of Montovia—and that worried her. Of course Princess Gemma's name on the Party Queens masthead brought kudos by the bucketload—and big-spending clients they might otherwise have struggled to attract. However, Gemma's incredible skills with food were sorely missed. Party Queens was all Eliza had in terms of income and interest. She needed to give the problem her full attention.

But Jake was proving the most enthralling of distractions.

She had stopped insisting on paying for her share of the activities he had scheduled for her. Much as she valued her independence, she simply couldn't afford a vacation Jake-style. Her wish to go snorkelling on the Great Barrier Reef had been granted—just her and

Jake on a privately chartered glass-bottom boat. Their games of golf had been eighteen holes on an exclusive private course with a waiting list for membership. Dinner was at secluded tables in booked-out restaurants.

Not that she was complaining at her sudden elevation in lifestyle, but there was a nagging feeling that she had again allowed herself to be taken over by a man. A charming man, yes, but controlling in his own quietly determined way.

When she'd protested Jake had said he was treating her, and wanted to make her vacation memorable. It would have seemed churlish to disagree. Just being with him was memorable enough—there was no doubt he was fabulous company. But she felt he was only letting her see the Jake he wanted her to see—which was frustrating. It was almost as if there were two different people: pre-divorce Jake and after-divorce Jake. After she'd spilled about her childhood, about her fears for the business, she'd expected some reciprocal confidences. There had been none but the most superficial.

On the afternoon of Day Four, after a long walk along the beach followed by a climb up the steep drive back home, Eliza was glad to dive into Jake's wet-edge pool. He did the same.

After swimming a few laps she rested back against him in the water, his arms around her as they both kicked occasionally to keep afloat. The water was the perfect temperature, and the last sunlight of the day filtered through the palm trees. Tropical birds flew around the trees, squawking among themselves as they settled for the evening. In the distance was the muted sound of the waves breaking on the beach below.

'This is utter bliss,' she said. 'My definition of heaven.'

The joy in her surroundings, in *him*, was bitter-sweet as it was about to end—but she couldn't share that thought with Jake. *This was just a four-day fling.*

'In that case you must be an angel who's flown down to keep me company,' he said.

'That's very poetic of you,' she said, twisting her head to see his face.

He grinned. 'I have my creative moments,' he replied as he dropped a kiss on her forehead.

It was a casual kiss she knew didn't mean anything other than to signify their ease with the very satisfying physical side of this vacation interlude.

'I could see *you* with a magnificent set of angel man wings, sprouting from your shoulder blades,' she said. 'White, tipped with gold.' *And no clothes at all.*

'All the better to fly you away with me,' he said. 'You must have wings too.'

'Blue and silver, I think,' she mused.

She enjoyed their light-hearted banter. After three days with him she didn't expect anything deeper or more meaningful. He was charming, fun, and she enjoyed being with him.

But he wasn't the Jake Marlowe who had so intrigued her with hints of hidden depths when she'd first met him. That Jake Marlowe had been as elusive as the last fleeting strains of the Strauss waltz lilting through the corridor as she had fled that ballroom in Montovia. She wondered if he had really existed outside her imagination. Had she been so smitten with his fallen angel looks that she'd thought there was more there for her than physical attraction?

'We did an angel-themed party a few months ago,' she said. 'That's what made me think about the wings.'

'You feasted on angel food cake, no doubt?'

'A magnificent celestial-themed supper was served,' she said. 'Star-shaped cookies, rainbow cupcakes, cloud-shaped meringues. Gemma planned it all from Montovia and Andie made sure it happened.'

The angel party had worked brilliantly. The next party, when Gemma had been too caught up with her royal duties to participate fully in the planning, hadn't had quite the same edge. Four days of vacation on, and Eliza was still no closer to finding a solution to the lack of Gemma's hands-on presence in the day-to-day running of the company. Party Queens was heading to crisis point.

'Clever Gemma,' said Jake. 'Tristan told me she's shaken up all the stodgy traditional menus served at the castle.'

'I believe she has,' Eliza said. 'She's instigated cooking programmes in schools, too. They're calling her the people's princess, she told me. Gemma's delighted.'

'No more than Tristan is delighted with Gemma.'

Gemma and Tristan had found true love. Whereas *she* had found just a diverting interlude with Jake. After the royal wedding both Gemma and Andie had expressed high hopes for romance between the best man and the bridesmaid. Eliza had denied any interest. But deep in Eliza's most secret heart she'd entertained the thought too. She couldn't help a sense of regret that it so obviously wasn't going to happen.

Idly, Eliza swished her toes around in the water. 'They call these wet-edge pools infinity pools, don't they? Because they stretch out without seeming to end?'

'That's right,' he said.

'In some way these four days of my vacation seemed to have gone on for ever. In another they've flown. Only this evening left.'

'Can you extend your break? By another day, perhaps?'

She shook her head. 'There's still the Gemma problem to solve. And there are some big winter parties lined up for the months ahead. I have back-to-back appointments for the day after I get back. Some of which took me weeks to line up.'

'That's what happens when you run a successful business,' he said.

'As you know only too well,' she said. Party Queens was insignificant on the corporate scale compared to *his* company.

'I'd have trouble squeezing in another day here, too,' Jake said. 'I'm out of the country a lot these days. Next week I fly to Minnesota in the United States, to meet with Walter Burton on a joint venture between him and Dominic in which I'm involved. My clients are all around the world. I'll be in Bangalore in India the following week. Singapore the week after that.'

'Are you ever home?' Her voice rose.

'Not often, these days. My absences were a bone of contention with my ex. She was probably right when she said that I didn't give her enough time.'

Eliza paused. 'It doesn't sound like you have any more time now.'

Jake took a beat to answer. 'Are you any different? Seems to me you're as career-orientated as I am. How much room does Party Queens leave for a man in your life?'

'Not much,' she admitted. She felt bad that she had

fielded so many phone calls while she'd been with him. But being a party planner wasn't a nine-to-five weekday-only enterprise. 'The business comes first, last and in between.'

It could be different! she screamed silently. *For the right man.* But was she being honest with herself? Could Jake be the right man?

'Seems to me we're both wedded to our careers,' he said slowly. 'To the detriment of anything else.'

'That's not true,' she said immediately. Then thought about it. 'Maybe. If neither of us can spare another day to spend here together when it's been so perfect.'

'That tells *me* something,' he said, his voice guarded.

Eliza swallowed hard against the truth of his words. The loss of *what might have been* hurt.

'It could be for the best,' she said, trying to sound matter of fact, but inwardly weeping over a lost opportunity.

She didn't know him any better than on Day One. His body, yes. His heart and soul—no. Disappointment stabbed deep that Jake hadn't turned out to be the man she'd expected him to be when he'd been whirling her around that fairytale ballroom.

Why had she ever hoped for more? When she thought about it, the whole thing with Jake hadn't seemed quite real. From the moonlit terrace in Montovia to the way he'd intercepted her at the airport and whisked her away to this awesome house perched high above the beach, it had all had an element of fantasy.

Jake held her for a long moment without replying. She could feel the thudding of his heart against her back. The water almost stilled around them, with only the occasional slap against the tiled walls of the pool. She had a heart-stopping feeling he was saying goodbye.

Finally he released her, then swam around her so he faced her, with her back to the edge of the pool. His hair was dark with water and slick to his head. Drops of water glistened on the smooth olive of his skin. Her heart contracted painfully at how handsome he looked. At how much she wanted him.

But although they got on so well, both in bed and out of it, it was all on the surface. Sex and fun. Nothing deeper had developed. She needed something more profound. She also needed a man who cared enough to make time to see her—and she him.

'Do you really think so?' he asked.

'Sometimes things are only meant to be for a certain length of time,' she said slowly. 'You can ruin them by wanting more.'

Jake's heart pounded as he looked down into Eliza's face. She'd pushed her wet hair back from her face, showing the perfect structure of her cheekbones, the full impact of her eyes. Water from the pool had dripped down over her shoulders to settle in drops on the swell of her breasts. The reality of Eliza in a bikini had way exceeded his early fantasies.

Eliza was everything he'd hoped she'd be and more. She was an extraordinary woman. They were compatible both in bed and out. They even enjoyed the same sports. But she'd been more damaged by her divorce than he had imagined. Not to mention by the tragedy of her inability to have a baby.

The entire time he'd felt he had to tread carefully around her, keeping the conversation on neutral topics, never digging too deep. For all her warmth and laughter and seeming openness, he sensed a prickly barrier around her. And then there was her insistence on answering her phone at all but their most intimate of moments. Eliza seemed so determined to keep her independence—there appeared little room for compromise. And if there was one lesson he'd learned from his marriage it was that compromise was required when two strong personalities came together as a couple.

She was no more ready for a serious relationship than he was.

Day Four was practically done and dusted—and so, it seemed, was his nascent relationship with Eliza.

And yet... He couldn't tolerate the thought of this being a final goodbye. There was still something about her that made him want to know more.

'We could catch up again some time, when we find ourselves in each other's cities,' he said.

'Absolutely.'

She said it with an obviously forced enthusiasm that speared through him.

'I'd like that.'

She placed her hand on his cheek, cool from the water, looked into his eyes. It felt ominously like a farewell.

'Jake, I'm so glad we did this.'

He had to clear his throat to speak. 'Me too,' he managed to choke out. There was a long pause during which the air seemed heavy with words unsaid before he spoke again. 'We have mutual friends. One day we might get the chance to take up where we left off.'

'Yes,' she said. 'That would be nice.'

Nice? Had all that passion and promise dwindled to *nice?*

Maybe that was what happened in this brave new world of newly single dating. Jake couldn't help a nagging sense of doubt that it should end like this. Had they missed a step somewhere?

'Jake, about our mutual friends...?' she said.

'Yes?' he said.

'I didn't tell them I'd met you here. Can Dominic be discreet?'

'He doesn't know we caught up with each other either.'

'Shall we keep it secret from them?' she asked. 'It would be easier.'

'As far as they're concerned we went our separate ways in Port Douglas,' he said.

He doubted Dominic would be surprised to hear it had turned out that way. He had warned Jake that, fond as he was of Eliza, she could be 'a tough little cookie'. Jake had thought there was so much more to her than that. Perhaps Dominic had been right.

'That's settled, then,' she said. There was an air of finality to her words.

Eliza swam to the wide, shallow steps of the pool, waded halfway up them, then turned back. Her petite body packed a powerfully sexy punch in her black bikini. High, firm breasts, a flat tummy and narrow waist flaring into rounded hips and a perfectly curved behind. Perhaps he'd read too much into this episode. *It was just physical—nothing more.* A fantasy fulfilled.

'I need to finish packing,' she said. 'Then I can enjoy our final dinner without worrying.'

That was it? 'Eliza, don't go just yet. I want to tell you—'

She paused, turned back to face him. Their gazes met for a long moment in the dying light of the day. Time seemed to stand still.

'I've booked a very good restaurant,' he said.

'I'll... I'll look forward to it,' she said. She took the final step out of the pool. 'Don't forget I have an early start in the morning.'

'I'll be ready to drive you to Cairns,' he said.

He dreaded taking that journey in reverse with her, when the journey here from the airport had been so full of promise and simmering sensuality. Tomorrow's journey would no doubt be followed by a stilted farewell at the airport.

'That's so good of you to offer,' she said with excess politeness. 'But I didn't cancel my return shuttle bus trip. It would be easier all round if we said goodbye here tomorrow morning.'

'You're sure, Eliza?' He made a token protest.

'Absolutely sure,' she said, heading towards the house without a backward glance.

Jake watched her, his hands fisted by his sides. He fancied blue angel wings unfurling as she prepared to fly right out of his life.

It was stupid of him ever to have thought things with Eliza could end any other way.

CHAPTER EIGHT

TEN WEEKS LATER Eliza sat alone in her car, parked on a street in an inner western suburb of Sydney, too shaken even to think about driving away from an appointment that had rocked her world. She clutched her keys in her hand, too unsteady to get the key into the ignition.

Eliza hated surprises. She liked to keep her life under control, with schedules and timetables and plans. Surprises had derailed her life on more than one occasion. Most notably the revelation that her burst appendix had left her infertile. But in this case the derailment was one that had charged her with sheer bubbling joy in one way and deep, churning anxiety in the other.

She was pregnant.

'It would take a miracle for you to get pregnant.'

Those had been her doctor's words when Eliza had told her of her list of symptoms. Words that had petered out into shock at the sight of a positive pregnancy test.

That miracle had happened in Port Douglas, with Jake—most likely the one time there had been a slip with their protection. Eliza hadn't worried. After all, she couldn't get pregnant.

Seemed she could.

And she had.

She laid her hand on her tummy, still flat and firm. But there was a tiny new life growing in there. *A baby.* She could hardly believe it was true, still marvelled at the miracle. But she had seen it.

Not *it.*

Him or her.

The doctor had wanted an ultrasound examination to make absolutely sure there wasn't an ectopic pregnancy in the damaged tube.

Active—like me, had been Eliza's first joyous thought when she'd seen the image of her tiny baby, turning cartwheels safe and sound inside her womb. Her second thought had been of loneliness and regret that there was no one there to share the miraculous moment with her. But she wanted this more than she had ever wanted anything in her life.

Her baby.

Eliza realised her cheeks were wet with tears. Fiercely, she scrubbed at her eyes.

Her third thought after the initial disbelief and shock had been to call Jake and tell him. There was absolutely no doubt he was the father.

His baby.

But how could she? He'd made it very clear he didn't *ever* want to be a father.

Dear heaven, she couldn't tell him.

He would think she was one of the dollar signs flashing gold-diggers he so despised. What had he said?

'A baby means lifetime child support—that's a guaranteed income for a certain type of woman.'

She dreaded the scorn in his eyes if she told him.

You know I told you I couldn't have a baby? Turns out I'm pregnant. You're going to be a daddy.

And what if he wanted her not to go forward with the pregnancy? No way—ever—would that be an option for her.

How on earth had this happened?

'Nature can be very persistent,' her doctor had explained. 'The tube we thought was blocked must not have been completely blocked. Or it unblocked itself.'

It really was a miracle—and one she hugged to herself.

She was not daunted by the thought of bringing the baby up by herself. Not that she believed it would be easy. But she owned her own home—a small terraced house in Alexandria, not far from the converted warehouse that housed the Party Queens headquarters. And Party Queens was still doing well financially, thanks to her sound management and the talent and drive of her business partners. And a creative new head chef was working out well. The nature of the business meant her hours could be flexible. Andie had often brought baby Hugo in when he was tiny, and did so even now, when he was a toddler. Eliza could afford childcare when needed—perhaps a nanny. Though she was determined to raise her child herself, with minimal help from nannies and childminders.

Her impossible dream had come true. *She was going to be a mother.* But the situation with her baby's father was more of a nightmare.

Eliza rested her head on her folded arms on top of the steering wheel, slumped with despair. *Pregnant from a four-night stand.* By a man she hadn't heard from since he'd walked her down the steep driveway that led away from his tropical hideaway and waved her goodbye.

Now he'd think she'd tried to trap him.

'I certainly wouldn't want to find myself caught in a trap like that,' he'd said, with a look of horror on his handsome face.

Eliza raised her head up off her folded arms. Took a few deep, steadying breaths. She wouldn't tell Jake. Nor would she tell her best friends about her pregnancy. Not yet. Not when both their husbands were friends with Jake.

If her tummy was this flat now, hopefully she wouldn't show for some time yet. Maybe she could fudge the dates. Or say the baby had been conceived by donor and IVF. The fact that Jake lived in Brisbane would become an advantage once she couldn't hide her pregnancy any longer. He wouldn't have to see her and her burgeoning bump.

But what if the baby looked like Jake? People close to Jake, like Andie and Dominic, would surely twig to the truth. *What if...what if...what if?* She covered her ears with her hands, as if to silence the questions roiling in her brain. But to no effect.

Was it fair *not* to tell him he was going to be a father? If she didn't make any demands on him surely he wouldn't believe she was a gold-digger? Maybe he would want to play some role in the baby's life. She wouldn't fight him if he did. It would be better for the baby. The baby who would become a child, a teenager, a person. A person with the right to know about his or her father.

It was all too much for her to deal with. She put her hand to her forehead, then over her mouth, suddenly feeling clammy and nauseous again.

The sickness had been relentless—so had the bone-deep exhaustion. She hadn't recognised them as symptoms of pregnancy. Why would she when she'd believed herself to be infertile?

Instead she had been worried she might have some terrible disease. Even when her breasts had started to become sensitive she had blamed it on a possible hormonal disturbance. She'd believed she couldn't conceive right up until the doctor's astonished words: *'You're pregnant.'*

But why would Jake—primed by both his own experience with women with flashing dollar signs in their eyes and the warnings of what sounded like a rabid divorce support group—believe her?

She was definitely in this on her own.

Eliza knew she would feel better if she could start making plans for her future as a single mother. Then she would feel more in control. But right now she had to track down the nearest bathroom. No wonder she had actually lost weight rather than put it on, with this morning, noon and night sickness that was plaguing her.

Party Queens was organising a party to be held in two weeks' time—the official launch of a new business venture of Dominic's in which Jake held a stake. No doubt she would see him there. But she would be officially on duty and could make their contact minimal. Though it would be difficult to deal with. And not just because of her pregnancy. She still sometimes woke in the night, realising she had been dreaming about Jake and full of regrets that it hadn't worked out between them.

CHAPTER NINE

THE NEARER JAKE got to Dominic's house in Sydney for the launch party, the drier his mouth and the more clammy his hands on the wheel of the European sports car he kept garaged there. Twelve weeks since he'd seen Eliza and he found himself feeling as edgy as an adolescent. Counting down the minutes until he saw her again.

The traffic lights stayed on red for too long and he drummed his fingers impatiently on the steering wheel.

For most of the time since their four-day fling in Port Douglas he'd been out of the country. *But she'd rarely been out of his mind.* Jake didn't like admitting to failure—but he'd failed dismally at forgetting her. From the get-go he'd had trouble accepting the finality of their fling.

The driveway up to his house in Port Douglas had never seemed so steep as that morning when he had trudged back up it after waving Eliza off on the shuttle bus. He'd pushed open his door to quiet and emptiness and a sudden, piercing regret. Her laughter had seemed to dance still on the air of the house.

No matter how much he'd told himself he was cool about the way his time had gone with her, he hadn't been able to help but think that by protecting himself he had talked himself out of something that might have been special. Cheated himself of the chance to be with a woman who might only come along once in a lifetime.

He'd had no contact with her at all since that morning, even though Party Queens were organising this evening's launch party. Dominic had done all the liaising with the party planners. Of course he had—he was married to the Design Director.

By the time he reached Dominic's house, Jake was decidedly on edge. He sensed Eliza's presence as soon as he was ushered through the door of Dominic's impressive mansion in the waterfront suburb of Vaucluse. Was it her scent? Or was it that his instincts were so attuned to Eliza they homed in on her even within a crowd? He heard the soft chime of her laughter even before he saw her. Excitement and anticipation stirred. Just seeing Eliza from a distance was enough to set his heart racing.

He stood at a distance after he'd found her, deep in conversation with a female journalist he recognised. This particular journalist had been the one to label Dominic—one of the most generous men Jake had ever known—with the title of 'Millionaire Miser'.

Andie and Party Queens had organised a party on Christmas Day two years ago that had dispelled *that* reputation. Planning that party was how Andie had met Dominic. And a week after Christmas Dominic had arranged a surprise wedding for Andie. Jake had flown down from Brisbane to be best man, and that wedding was where he'd met Eliza for the first time.

Jake looked through the wall of French doors that

opened out from the ballroom of Dominic's grand Art Deco house to the lit-up garden and swimming pool beyond. He remembered his first sight of Eliza, exquisite in a flowing pale blue bridesmaid's dress, white flowers twisted through her dark hair. She had laughed up at him as they'd shared in the conspiracy of it all: the bride had had no idea of her own upcoming nuptials.

Jake had been mesmerised by Eliza's extraordinary blue eyes, captivated by her personality. They had chatted the whole way through the reception. He'd been separated from Fern at that stage, but still trying to revive something that had been long dead. Not wanting to admit defeat. Eliza had helped him see how pointless that was—helped him to see hope for a new future just by being Eliza.

Now she wasn't aware that he was there, and he watched her as she chatted to the journalist, her face animated, her smile at the ready. She was so lovely—and not just in looks. He couldn't think of another person whose company he enjoyed more than Eliza's. *Why had he let her go?*

He couldn't bear it if he didn't get some kind of second chance with her. He'd tried to rid himself of the notion that he was a one-woman man. After all, a billionaire bachelor was spoiled for choice. He didn't have to hunt around to find available woman—they found *him.* Theoretically, he could date a string of them—live up to his media reputation. Since Port Douglas he'd gone out with a few women, both in Australia and on his business travels. Not one had captured his interest. None had come anywhere near Eliza.

Tonight she looked every inch the professional, but with a quirky touch to the way she was dressed that was perfectly appropriate to her career as a party planner. She wore a full-skirted black dress, with long, tight, sheer sleeves, and high-heeled black stilettos. Her hair was twisted up behind her head and finished with a flat black velvet bow. What had she called her style? Retro-inspired? He would call the way she dressed 'ladylike'. But she was as smart and as business-savvy as any guy in a suit and necktie.

Did she feel the intensity of his gaze on her? She turned around, caught his eye. Jake smiled and nodded a greeting, not wanting to interrupt her conversation. He was shocked by her reaction. Initially a flash of delight lightened her face, only to be quickly replaced by wariness and then a conscious schooling of her features into polite indifference.

Jake felt as if he had been kicked in the gut. *Why?* They'd parted on good terms. He'd even thought he'd seen a hint of tears glistening in her eyes as she'd boarded the shuttle bus in Port Douglas. They'd both been aware that having mutual friends would mean they'd bump into each other at some stage. She must have known he would be here tonight—he was part of the proceedings.

He strode towards her, determined to find out what was going on. Dismissing him, she turned back to face the journalist. Jake paused mid-stride, astounded at her abruptness. Then it twigged. Eliza didn't want this particular newshound sniffing around for an exclusive featuring the billionaire bachelor and the party planner.

Jake changed direction to head over to the bar.

He kept a subtle eye on Eliza. As soon as she was free he headed towards her, wanting to get her attention before anyone else beat him to it.

'Hello,' he said, for all the world as if they weren't anything other than acquaintances with mutual friends. He dropped a kiss on her cool, politely offered cheek.

'Jake,' Eliza said.

This was Eliza the Business Director of Party Queens speaking. Not Eliza the lover, who had been so wonderfully responsive in his arms. Not Eliza his golfing buddy from Port Douglas, nor Eliza his bikini-clad companion frolicking in the pool.

'So good that you could make it down from Brisbane,' the Business Director said. 'This is a momentous occasion.'

'Indeed,' he said.

Momentous because it was the first time they'd seen each other after their four-day fling? More likely she meant it was momentous because it was to mark the occasion not only of the first major deal of Dominic's joint venture with the American billionaire philanthropist Walter Burton, but also the setting up the Sydney branch of Dominic's charity, The Underground Help Centre, for homeless young people.

'Walter Burton is here from Minnesota,' Eliza said. 'I believe you visited with him recently.'

'He flew in this morning,' he said.

Jake had every right to be talking to Eliza. He was one of the principals of the deal they were celebrating tonight. Party Queens was actually in *his* employ.

However, when that pushy journalist's eyes narrowed with interest and her steps slowed as she walked by him and Eliza, Jake remembered she'd been in Montovia to report on the royal wedding. As best man and bridesmaid, he and Eliza had featured in a number of photo shoots and articles. If it was rumoured they'd had an affair—and that was all it had been—it would be big tabloid news.

He gritted his teeth. There was something odd here. Something else. Eliza's reticence could not be put down just to the journalist's presence.

Jake leaned down to murmur in her ear, breathed in her now familiar scent, sweet and intoxicating. 'It's good to see you. I'd like to catch up while I'm in Sydney.'

Eliza took a step back from him. 'Sorry—not possible,' she said. She gave an ineffectual wave to indicate the room, now starting to fill up with people. The action seemed extraordinarily lacking in Eliza's usual energy. 'This party is one of several that are taking up all my time.'

So what had changed? Work had always seemed to come first with Eliza. Whereas *he* was beginning to see it shouldn't. That there should be a better balance to life.

'I understand,' he said. But he didn't. 'What about after the party? Catch up for coffee at my apartment at the wharf?' He owned a penthouse apartment in a prestigious warehouse conversion right on the harbour in inner eastern Sydney.

Eliza's lashes fluttered and she couldn't meet his eyes. 'I'm sorry,' she said again. 'I… I'm not in the mood for company.'

Jake was too flabbergasted to say anything. He eventually found the words. 'You mean not in the mood for *me*?'

She lifted her chin, looked up at him. For once he couldn't read the expression in those incredible blue eyes. Defiance? Regret? *Fear?* It both puzzled and worried him.

'Jake, we agreed to four days only.'

The sentence sounded disconcertingly well-rehearsed. A shard of pain stabbed him at her tone.

'We left open an option to meet again, did we not?' He asked the question, but he thought he could predict the answer.

She put her hand on her heart and then indicated him in an open-palmed gesture that would normally have indicated togetherness. 'Me. You. We tried it. It…it didn't work.'

The slight stumble on her words alerted him to a shadow of what looked like despair flitting across her face. *What was going on?*

'I don't get it.' Jake was noted for his perseverance. He wouldn't give up on Eliza easily.

A spark of the feisty Eliza he knew—or thought he knew—flashed through.

'Do I have to analyse it? Isn't it enough that I just don't want to be with you again?'

He didn't believe her. Not when he remembered her unguarded expression when she'd first noticed him this evening.

There was something not right here.

Or was he being arrogant in his disbelief that Eliza simply didn't want him in her life? That the four days had proved he wasn't what she wanted? Was he falling back into his old ways? Unable to accept that a woman he wanted no longer wanted *him*? That wanting to persevere with Eliza was the same kind of blind stubbornness that had made him hang on to a marriage in its death throes—to the ultimate misery of both him and his ex-wife? Not to mention the plummeting profit margins of his company—thankfully now restored.

'Is there someone else?' he asked.

A quick flash of something in her eyes made him pay close attention to her answer.

'Someone else? No. Not really.'

'What do you mean "not really"?'

'Bad choice of words. There's no other man.'

He scrutinised her face. Noticed how pale she looked, with dark shadows under her eyes and a new gauntness to her cheekbones. Her lipstick was a red slash against her pallor. More colour seemed to leach from her face as she spoke.

'Jake. There's no point in going over this. It's over between us. Thank you for understanding.' She suddenly snatched her hand to her mouth. 'I'm afraid I have to go.'

Without another word she rushed away, heading out of the ballroom and towards the double arching stairway that was a feature of the house.

Jake was left staring after her. Dumbfounded. Stricken with a sudden aching sense of loss.

He knew he had to pull himself together as he saw Walter Burton heading for him. He pasted a smile on his face. Extended his hand in greeting.

The older man, with his silver hair and perceptive pale eyes, pumped his hand vigorously. 'Good to see you, Jake. I'm having fun here, listening to people complain that it's cold for June. Winter in Sydney is a joke. I'm telling them they don't know what winter is until they visit Minnesota in February.'

'Of course,' Jake said.

He was trying to give Walter his full attention,

but half his mind was on Eliza as he looked over the heads of the people who now surrounded him, nodded vaguely at guests he recognised. *Where had she gone?*

Walter's eyes narrowed. 'Lady trouble?' he observed.

'Not really,' Jake said. He didn't try to deny that Eliza was his lady. Dominic and Andie had had to stage a fake engagement because of this older man's moral stance. He found himself wishing Eliza really was his lady, with an intensity that hurt so much he nearly doubled over.

'Don't worry, son, it'll pass over,' Walter said. 'They get that way in the first months. You know…a bit erratic. It gets better.'

Jake stared at him. 'What do you mean?'

'When a woman's expecting she—'

Jake put up his hand. 'Whoa. I don't know where you're going with this, Walter. Expecting? Not Eliza. She…she can't have children.' And Eliza certainly didn't *look* pregnant in that gorgeous black dress.

'Consider me wrong, then. But I've had six kids and twice as many grandkids.' Walter patted his rather large nose with his index finger. 'I've got an instinct for when a woman's expecting. Sometimes I've known before she was even aware herself. I'd put money on it that your little lady is in the family way. I'm sorry for jumping the gun if she hasn't told you yet.'

Reeling, Jake managed to change the subject. But Walter's words kept dripping through his mind like the most corrosive of acids.

Had she tricked him? His fists clenched by his sides. Eliza? A scheming gold-digger? Trying to trap him with the oldest trick in the book? She had sounded so convincing when she'd told him about the burst appendix and her subsequent infertility. Was it all a lie? If so, what else had she lied about?

He felt as if everything he'd believed in was falling away from him.

Then he was hit by another, equally distressing thought. If she wasn't pregnant, was she ill?

One thing was for sure—she was hiding something from him. And he wouldn't be flying back to Brisbane until he found out what it was.

CHAPTER TEN

JAKE USUALLY NEVER had trouble sleeping. But late on
the night of the launch party, back in his waterfront
apartment, he tossed and turned. The place was luxurious, but lonely. He'd had high hopes of bringing
Eliza back here this evening. To talk, to try and come
to some arrangement so he could see more of her. If
they'd ended up in bed that would have been good too.
He hadn't been with anyone else since her. Had recoiled
from kissing the women he'd dated.

Thoughts of his disastrous encounter with her kept
him awake for what seemed like most of the night.
And then there was Walter's observation to nag at him.
Finally, at dawn, he gave up on sleep and went for a
run. Vigorous physical activity helped his thought pro-
cesses, he'd always found.

In the chill of early morning he ran up past the im-
posing Victorian buildings of the New South Wales
Art Gallery and through the public green space of The
Domain.

He paused to do some stretches at the end of the pen-
insula at Mrs Macquarie's Chair—a bench cut into a
sandstone slab where it was reputed a homesick early
governor's wife had used to sit and watch for sailing

ships coming from Great Britain. The peaceful spot gave a panoramic view of Sydney Harbour: the 'coat hanger' bridge and the white sails of the Opera House. Stray clouds drifting around the buildings were tinted pink from the rising sun.

Jake liked Sydney and thought he could happily live in this city. Brisbane seemed all about the past. In fact he was thinking about moving his company's headquarters here. He had wanted to talk to Eliza about that, to put forward the idea that such a move would mean he'd be able to see more of her if they started things up between them again. Not much point now.

The pragmatic businessman side of Jake told him to wipe his hands of her and walk away. Eliza had made it very clear she didn't want him around. A man who had graduated from a dating after divorce workshop would know to take it on the chin, cut his losses and move on. After all, they'd only been together for four days, three months ago.

But the more creative, intuitive side of him, which had guided him through decisions that had made him multiple millions, wouldn't let him off that easily. Even if she'd lied to him, tricked him, deceived him—and that was only a suspicion at this stage—he had a strong feeling that she needed him. And he needed to find out what was going on.

He'd never got a chance to chat with her again at the party—she had evaded him and he'd had official duties to perform. But he'd cancelled his flight back to Brisbane, determined to confront her today.

Jake ran back home, showered, changed, ate breakfast. Predictably, Eliza didn't reply to his text and her phone went to voicemail. He called the Party Queens headquarters to be told Eliza was working at home today. Okay, so he would visit her at home—and soon.

He hadn't been to Eliza's house before, but he knew where it was. Investment-wise, she'd been canny. She'd bought a worker's terraced cottage in an industrial area of the inner city just before a major push to its gentrification. The little house, attached on both sides, looked immaculately restored and maintained. Exactly what he'd expect from Eliza.

It sat on one level, with a dormer window in the roof, indicating that she had probably converted the attic. External walls were painted the colour of natural sandstone, with windows and woodwork picked out in white and shades of grey. The tiny front garden was closed off from the sidewalk by a black wrought-iron fence and a low, perfectly clipped hedge.

Jake pushed open the shiny black gate and followed the black-and-white-tiled path. He smiled at the sight of the front door, painted a bold glossy red to match the large red planter containing a spiky-leaved plant. Using the quaint pewter knocker shaped like a dragonfly, he rapped on the door.

He heard footsteps he recognised as Eliza's approaching the door. They paused while, he assumed, she checked out her visitor through the peephole. Good. He was glad she was cautious about opening her door to strangers.

The pause went on for rather too long. Was she going to ignore him? He would stay here all day if he had to. He went to rap again but, with his hand still on its knocker, the door opened and she was there.

Jake didn't often find himself disconcerted to the

point of speechlessness. But he was too shocked to greet her.

This was an Eliza he hadn't seen before: hair dishevelled, face pale and strained with smudges of last night's make-up under her eyes. But what shocked him most was her body. Dark grey yoga pants and a snug pale grey top did nothing to disguise the small but definite baby bump. Her belly was swollen and rounded.

Eliza's shoulders slumped, and when she looked up at him her eyes seemed weary and dulled by defeat. In colour more denim than sapphire.

She took a deep breath and the rising of her chest showed him that her breasts were larger too. The dress she'd worn the previous night had hidden everything.

'Yes, I'm pregnant. Yes, it's yours. No, I won't be making any claims on you.'

Jake didn't mean to blurt out his doubt so baldly, but out it came. 'I thought you couldn't conceive.'

'So did I. That I'm expecting a baby came as a total surprise.' She gestured for him to follow her. 'Come in. Please. This isn't the kind of conversation I want to have in the street.'

The cottage had been gutted and redesigned into an open usable space, all polished floors and white walls. It opened out through a living area, delineated by carefully placed furniture, to a kitchen and eating area. Two black cats lay curled asleep on a bean bag, oblivious to the fact that Eliza had company. At the back, through a wall of folding glass doors, he saw a small courtyard with paving and greenery. A staircase—more sculpture than steps—led up to another floor. The house was furnished in a simple contemporary style, with carefully placed paintings and ornaments that at another time Jake might have paused to examine.

'I need to sit down,' Eliza said, lowering herself onto the modular sofa, pushing a cushion behind her back, sighing her relief.

'Are you okay?' Jake asked, unable to keep the concern from his voice. A sudden urge to protect her pulsed through him. But it was as if there was an invisible barrier flashing *Don't Touch* around her. The dynamic between them was so different it was as if they were strangers again. He hated the feeling. Somehow he'd lost any connection he'd had with her, without realising how or why.

She gave that same ineffectual wave she'd made the night before. It was as if she were operating at half-speed—like an appliance running low on battery. 'Sit down. Please. You towering over me is making me feel dizzy.'

She placed her hand on her bump in a protective gesture he found both alien and strangely moving.

He sat down on the sofa opposite her. 'Morning sickness?' he asked warily. He wasn't sure how much detail he'd get in reply. And he was squeamish about illness and female things—very squeamish.

'I wish,' she said. 'It's non-stop nausea like I couldn't have imagined. All day. All night.' She closed her eyes for a moment and shook her head before opening them again. 'I feel utterly drained.'

Jake frowned. 'That doesn't sound right. Have you seen your doctor?'

'She says some women suffer more than others and nausea is a normal part of pregnancy. Though it's got much worse since I last saw the doctor.' She grimaced.

'But it's worth it. Anything is worth it. I never thought I could have a baby.'

'So what happened? I mean, how—?'

She linked her hands together on her lap. 'I can see doubt in your eyes, Jake. I didn't lie to you. I genuinely believed I was infertile. Sterile. Barren. All those things my ex called me, as if it was my fault. But I'm not going to pretend I'm anything but thrilled to be having this baby. I… I don't expect you to be.'

Jake had believed in Eliza's honesty and integrity. She had sounded so convincing when she'd told him about her ruptured appendix and the damage it had caused. Her personal tragedy. And yet suddenly she was pregnant. Could a man be blamed for wanting an explanation?

'So what happened to allow—?' He couldn't find a word that didn't sound either clinical or uncomfortably personal.

'My doctor described it as a miracle. Said that a microscopic-sized channel clear in a sea of scar tissue must have enabled it to happen. I can hardly believe it myself.' A hint of a wan smile tilted the corners of her mouth. 'Though the nausea never allows me to forget.'

'Are you sure—?'

She leaned forward. 'Sure I'm pregnant? Absolutely. Up until my tummy popped out it was hard to believe.' She stilled. Pressed her lips together so hard they became colourless. 'You didn't mean that, did you? You meant am I sure the baby is yours.'

Her eyes clouded with hurt. Jake knew he had said inextricably the wrong thing. Though it seemed reasonable for him to want to be sure. He *still* thought it was reasonable to ask. They'd had a four-day fling and he hadn't heard a word from her since.

'I didn't mean—'

Her face crumpled. 'Yes, you did. For the record, I'll tell you there was no one else. There had been no one else for a long time and has been no one since. But feel free to ask for a DNA test if you want proof.'

He moved towards her. 'Eliza, I—'

Abruptly she got up from the sofa. Backed away from him. 'Don't come near me. Don't touch me. Don't quote your dating after divorce handbook that no doubt instructs you about the first question to ask of a scheming gold-digger trying to trap you.'

'Eliza, I'm sorry. I—'

She shrugged with a nonchalance he knew was an absolute sham.

'You didn't know me well at Port Douglas,' she said. 'I could have bedded a hundred guys over the crucial time for conception for all you knew. It's probably a question many men would feel justified in asking under the circumstances. But not *you* of *me*. Not after I'd been straightforward with you. Not when we have close friends in common. A relationship might not have worked for us. But I thought there was mutual respect.'

'There was. There is. Of course you're upset. Let me—'

'I'm not *upset*. I'm *disappointed*, if anything. Disappointed in *you*. Again, for the record, I will not ask anything of you. Not money. Not support. Certainly not your name on the birth certificate. I am quite capable of doing this on my own. *Happy* to do this on my own. I have it all planned and completely under control. You can just walk out that door and forget you ever knew me.'

Jake had no intention of leaving. If indeed this baby was his—and he had no real reason to doubt her—he would not evade his responsibilities. But before he had a chance to say anything further Eliza groaned.

'Oh, no. Not again.'

She slapped her hand over her mouth, pushed past him and ran towards the end of the house and, he assumed, the bathroom.

He waited for what seemed like a long time for her to do what she so obviously had to do. Until it began to seem too long. Worried, he strode through the living room to find her. That nagging sense that she needed him grew until it consumed him.

'Eliza! Answer me!' he called, his voice raw with urgency.

'I… I'm okay.' Her voice, half its usual volume, half its usual clarity, came from behind a door to his left.

The door slowly opened. Eliza put one foot in front of the other in an exaggerated way to walk unsteadily out. She clutched the doorframe for support.

Jake sucked in a breath of shock at how ashen and weak she looked. Beads of perspiration stood out on her forehead. He might not be a doctor, but every instinct told him this was not right. 'Eliza. Let me help you.'

'You…you're still here?' she said. 'I told you to leave.'

'I'm not going anywhere.'

'There…there's blood.' Her voice caught. 'There shouldn't be blood. I… I don't know what to do. Can you call Andie for me, please?'

Jake felt gutted that he was right there and yet not the first person she'd sought to help her.

She wanted him gone.

No way was he leaving her.

He took her elbow to steady her. She leaned into him and he was stunned at how thin she'd become since he'd last held her in his arms. Pregnant women were meant to put *on* weight, not lose it. *Something was very wrong.*

Fear grabbed his gut. He mustn't let her sense it. Panic would make it worse. She felt so fragile, as if she might break if he held her too hard. Gently he lifted her and carried her to a nearby chair. She moaned as he settled her into it.

She cradled her head in her hands. 'Headache. Now I've got a headache.' Her voice broke into a sob.

Jake realised she was as terrified as he was. He pulled out his phone.

'Call Andie...' Her voice trailed away as she slumped into the chair.

He supported her with his body as he started to punch out a number with fingers that shook. 'I'm not calling Andie. I'm calling an ambulance,' he said, his voice rough with fear.

CHAPTER ELEVEN

WHEN ELIZA WOKE up in a hospital bed later that day, the first thing she saw was Jake sprawled in a chair near her bed. He was way too tall for the small chair and his long, blue-jeans-clad legs were flung out in front of him. His head was tilted back, his eyes closed. His hair looked as if he'd combed it through with his hands and his black T-shirt was crumpled.

She gazed at him for a long moment. Had a man ever looked so good? Her heart seemed to skip a beat. Last time she had seen him asleep he had been beside her in his bed at Port Douglas on Day Three. She had awoken him with a trail of hungry little kisses that had delighted him. Now here he was in a visitor's chair in a hospital room. She was pregnant and he had doubts that the baby was his. How had it come to this?

Eliza had only vague memories of the ambulance trip to the hospital. She'd been drifting in and out of consciousness. What she did remember was Jake by her side. Holding her hand the entire time. Murmuring a constant litany of reassurance. *Being there for her.*

She shifted in the bed. A tube had been inserted in the back of her left hand and she was attached to a drip. Automatically her hand went to her tummy. She was still getting used to the new curve where it had always been flat.

Jake opened his eyes, sat forward in his chair. 'You're awake.' His voice was underscored with relief.

'So are you. I thought you were asleep.' Her voice felt croaky, her throat a little sore.

He got up and stood by her bed, looked down to where her hand remained on her tummy. The concern on his face seemed very real.

'I don't know what you remember about this morning,' he said. 'But the baby is okay. *You're* okay.'

'I remember the doctor telling me. Thank heaven. And seeing the ultrasound. I couldn't have borne it if—'

'You'd ruptured a blood vessel. The baby was never at risk.'

She closed her eyes, opened them again. 'I felt so dreadful. I thought I must be dying. And I was so worried for the baby.'

'Severe dehydration was the problem,' he said.

She felt at a disadvantage, with him towering so tall above her. 'I can see how that happened. I hadn't even been able to keep water down. The nausea was so overwhelming. It's still there, but nothing like as bad.'

'Not your everyday morning sickness, according to your doctor here. An extreme form known as *Hyperemesis gravidarum.* Same thing that put the Duchess of Cambridge in hospital with her pregnancies, so a nurse told me.'

He sounded both knowledgeable and concerned. Jake here with her? The billionaire bachelor acting nurse? How had this happened?

'A lot of the day is a blur,' she said. 'But I remember the doctor telling me that. No wonder I felt so bad.'

'You picked up once the doctors got you on intravenous fluids.'

She raised her left wrist and looked up at the clear plastic bag hooked over a stand above. 'I'm still on them, by the looks of it.'

'You have to stay on the drip for twenty-four hours. They said you need vitamins and nutrients as well as fluids.'

Eliza reeled at the thought of Jake conversing with the doctors, discussing her care. It seemed surreal that he should be here, like this. 'How do you know all this? In fact, how come you're in my room?' Eliza didn't want to sound ungrateful. But she had asked him to leave her house. Though it was just as well he hadn't, as it had turned out.

'I admitted you to the hospital. They asked about my relationship to you. I told them I was your partner and the father of the baby. On those terms, it's quite okay for me to be in your room.'

'Oh,' she said. She slumped back on the pillows. Their conversation of this morning came flooding back. How devastated she'd felt when he'd asked if she sure he was the father. 'Even though you don't actually think the baby is yours?' she said dully.

He set his jaw. 'I never said that. I believed you couldn't get pregnant. You brushed me off at the party. Didn't tell me anything—refused to see me. Then I discovered you were pregnant. It's reasonable I would have been confused as to the truth. Would want to be sure.'

'Perhaps,' she conceded.

It hurt that his first reaction had been distrust. But she had no right to feel a sense of betrayal—they'd had a no-strings fling. They'd been lovers with no commitment whatsoever. And he was a man who had made it very clear he never wanted children.

'I believe you when you say the baby is mine, Eliza. It's unexpected. A shock. But I have no reason to doubt you.'

Eliza was so relieved at his words she didn't know what to say and had to think about her response. 'I swear you *are* the father. I would never deceive you about something so important.'

'Even about the hundred other men?' he said, with a hint of a smile for the first time.

She managed a tentative smile in return. 'There was only ever you.'

'I believe you,' he said.

'You don't want DNA testing to be certain? Because I—'

'No,' he said. 'Your word is enough.'

Eliza nodded, too overcome to say anything. She knew how he felt about mercenary gold-diggers. But the sincerity in his eyes assured her that he no longer put her in that category. If, indeed, he ever had. Perhaps she had been over-sensitive. But that didn't change the fact that he didn't want to be a father.

'I don't want to be a father—ever.'

How different this could have been in a different universe—where they were a couple, had planned the child, met the result of her pregnancy test with mutual joy. But that was as much a fantasy as those frozen in time moments of him whirling her around in a waltz, when the future had still been full of possibilities for Eliza and Jake.

Now here he was by her bedside, acting the concerned friend. She shouldn't read anything else into his care of her. Jake had only done for her what he would have done for any other woman he'd found ill and alone.

Eliza felt a physical ache at how much she still wanted him. She wondered—not for the first time—if she would *ever* be able to turn off her attraction to him. But physical attraction wasn't enough—no matter how good the sex. A domineering workaholic, hardly ever in the same country as her, was scarcely the man she would have chosen as the father of her child. Though his genes were good.

'Thank you for calling the ambulance and checking me in to the hospital,' she said. 'And thank you for staying with me. But can I ask you one more thing, please?' *Before we say goodbye.*

'Of course,' he said.

'Can you ask the hospital staff to fix their mistake with my room?' She looked around her. The room was more like a luxurious hotel suite than a hospital room. 'I'm not insured for a private room. They'll need to move me to a shared ward.'

'There's been no mistake,' he said. 'I've taken responsibility for paying your account.'

Eliza stared at him. '*What?* You can't do that,' she said.

'As far as the hospital is concerned I am the baby's father. I pay the bills.'

Eliza gasped. This wasn't right. She needed to keep control over her pregnancy and everything involved with it. 'That was a nice gesture, but I can't possibly accept your offer,' she said.

'You don't have a choice,' he said. 'It's already done.'

Eliza had never felt more helpless, lying in a hospital bed tied up to a drip and monitors. It wasn't a feeling she was used to. 'Jake, please don't make me argue over this.' She was feeling less nauseous, but she'd been told she had to avoid stress and worry as well as keep up fluids and nourishment. 'What happened to you keeping your credit cards in your wallet when it comes to me?'

'You can't have it both ways, Eliza. You want me to acknowledge paternity? That means I take financial responsibility for your care. It's not negotiable.'

This was the controlling side of Jake that had made her wary of him for more than a no-strings fling. 'You don't make decisions for me, Jake. I will not—'

At that moment a nurse came into the room to check on Eliza's drip and to take her temperature and blood pressure. Jake stepped back from the bed and leaned against the wall to let the nurse get on with what she needed to do.

'She's looking so much better now than when you brought her in,' the nurse said.

'Thankfully,' said Jake. 'I was very worried about her.'

Eliza fumed. The nurse was addressing Jake and talking about her as if she was some inanimate object. 'Yes, I *am* feeling much better,' she said pointedly to the nurse. But Jake's smile let her know he knew exactly what was going on—and found it amusing. Which only made Eliza fume more.

'That's what we want to hear,' said the nurse with

a cheerful smile, seemingly oblivious to the under-currents.

She was no doubt well meaning, but Eliza felt she had to assert herself. It was *her* health. *Her* baby. Under *her* control. 'When can I go home?' Eliza asked.

The nurse checked her chart. 'You have to be on the intravenous drip for a total of twenty-four hours.'

'So I can go home tomorrow morning?'

'If the doctor assesses you as fit to be discharged. Of course you can't leave by yourself, and there has to be someone at home to care for you.'

'That's okay,' said Jake, before Eliza could say anything. 'I'll be taking her home and looking after her.'

The nurse smiled. 'That's settled, then.'

'No, it's not. I—' Eliza protested.

'Thank you,' said Jake to the nurse.

Eliza waited until the nurse had left the room. 'What was that about?' she hissed.

Jake moved back beside her bed. 'I'll be picking you up when you're discharged from hospital tomorrow. We can talk about whether you'd like me to stay with you for a few days or whether I organise a nurse.'

She had to tilt her head back to confront him. 'Or how about I look after myself?' she said.

'That's not an option,' said Jake. 'Unless you want to stay longer in hospital. *Hyperemesis gravidarum* is serious. You have to keep the nausea under control and get enough nourishment for both your health and your baby's sake. You know all this. The doctor has told you that you're still weak.'

'That doesn't mean *you* have to take over, Jake.'

Eliza felt she was losing control of the situation and

she didn't like it one bit. At the same time she didn't want to do anything to risk harming the baby.

'You have another choice,' he said. 'You could move in with Andie. She's offered to have you to stay with her and Dominic.'

'You've spoken to Andie? But she doesn't know—'

'That you're pregnant? She does now. You asked me to call her this morning. So I did while you were asleep.'

'What did she say?' Andie would not appreciate being left out of the loop.

'She was shocked to find out you and I had had an affair and you'd kept it from her. And more than a little hurt that you didn't take her into your confidence about your pregnancy.'

'I would have, but I didn't want her telling...'

'Telling me?'

'That's right.'

'If I'd flown back to Brisbane this morning instead of coming to see you would you have *ever* told me?' His mouth was set in a grim line.

'I wasn't thinking that far ahead. I just didn't want you to think I was trying to trap you into something you didn't want. You were so vehement about gold-diggers. I... I couldn't bear the thought of seeing disgust in your eyes when you looked at me.'

'You will *never* see disgust in my eyes when it comes to you, Eliza,' he said. 'Disbelief that you would try to hide this from me, but not disgust. We have mutual friends. I would have heard sooner or later.'

'I would rather it had been later. I didn't want you trying to talk me out of it.'

The look of shock on his face told her she might have said the wrong thing.

'I would never have done that,' he said.

She realised how out-of-the-blue her situation had been for him. And how well he was handling it.

'I wasn't to know,' she said. 'After all, we hardly know each other.'

For a long moment Jake looked into her face—searching for what she didn't know.

Finally he spoke. 'That's true. But there should be no antagonism between us. Here isn't the time or the place to discuss how we'll deal with the situation on an ongoing basis.' He glanced down at his watch. 'Andie will be here to visit you soon. I'm going to go. I'll see you in the morning.'

Eliza's feelings were all over the place. She didn't know whether she could blame hormones for the tumult of her emotions. No way did she want Jake—or any other man—controlling her, telling her what to do with her life. But she had felt so safe and comforted with him by her side today. Because while her pregnancy had changed the focus of everything, it didn't change the attraction she'd felt for Jake from the get-go. He had been wonderful to her today. She wished she could beg him to stay.

'Before you leave, let me thank you again for your help today, Jake. I can't tell you how much I appreciate you being with me.'

'You're welcome,' he said. 'I'm just glad you're okay. And so glad I called by to your house this morning.'

She sat up straighter in an attempt to bring him closer. Put out her hand and placed it on his arm. 'I'm sorry,' she said. 'Not sorry about the baby—my mira-

cle baby. But sorry our carefree fling had such conse-
quences and that we've been flung back together again
in such an awkward situation.'

'No need to apologise for that,' he said gruffly.

Jake kept up the brave front until he was out of the hospital and on the pavement. He felt totally strung out
from the events of the last day. Everything had happened so quickly. He needed time to think it through
and process it.

Thank heaven he hadn't encountered Andie on the
way out. He'd liked Andie from the moment Dominic
had first introduced him to her, on the day of their surprise wedding. Each time he met his friend's wife he
liked her more. Not in a romantic way—although she
was undoubtedly gorgeous. He liked the way Andie
made his best friend so happy after the rotten hand
life had dealt Dominic when it came to love. If Jake
had had a sister, he would have wanted her to be just
like Andie.

But Andie told it how it was. And Eliza was her
dearest friend, whom she would defend with every
weapon at hand. Jake wouldn't have appreciated a face-
to-face confrontation with her on the steps of the hospital. Not when he was feeling so on edge. Not after the
conversation he'd already had with her on the phone.

When he'd called to tell her Eliza was in hospital Andie been shocked to hear the reason. Shocked
and yet thrilled for Eliza, as she knew how much her
friend had wanted to have children but had thought
she couldn't conceive.

'This is a miracle for her!' Andie had exclaimed,
and had promptly started to sob on the phone. Which

had been further proof—not that he'd needed it—that Eliza had not been lying. Then, in true sisterly fashion, Andie had hit Jake with some advice. Advice he hadn't thought he'd needed but he'd shut up and listened.

'Don't you hurt her, Jake,' she'd said, her voice still thick with tears. 'I had no idea you two had had a…a thing. Eliza is Party Queens family. *You're* family. She thinks she's so strong and independent, but this pregnancy will make her vulnerable. She's not some casual hook-up girl. You can't just write a cheque and walk away.'

'It's not like that—' he'd started to protest. But the harsh truth of it, put into words, had hit him like blows to the gut.

Eliza was connected to his life through his best friends, Dominic and Tristan, and their wives. He could argue all he liked that their fling had been a mutually convenient scratching of the itch of their attraction. But that sounded so disrespectful to Eliza. In his heart he knew he'd wanted much more time with her. Which was why he had been considering a move to Sydney. But Eliza's pregnancy had put everything on a very different footing.

Andie had continued. 'Oh, what the heck? This is none of my business. You're a big boy. *You* figure out what Eliza needs. And give it to her in spades.'

Jake was beginning to see what Eliza needed. And also what *he* needed. He'd never been so scared than when she'd passed out on the chair while they were waiting for the ambulance to arrive. In a moment of stricken terror he'd thought he was going to lose her. And it had hit him with the power of a sledgehammer hurtling towards his head how much she had come to mean to him—as a friend as well as a lover. Suddenly a life without Eliza in it in some way had become untenable.

But the phone call with Andie wasn't what had him still staggering, as if that sledgehammer really had connected. It was the baby.

First he'd been hit with the reality of absorbing the fact that Eliza was expecting a baby—and the realisation that it had irrevocably changed things between them. Then he'd been stricken by seeing Eliza so frighteningly ill. But all that had been eclipsed by the events at the hospital.

Once the medical team had stabilised Eliza with fluids—she'd been conscious enough to refuse any anti-nausea medication—they'd wheeled her down, with him in attendance, to have an ultrasound to check that all was well with her developing foetus.

The technician had covered Eliza's bump with a jelly—cold, and it had made her squeal—and then pressed an electronic wand over her bump. The device had emitted high-frequency soundwaves that had formed an image when they'd come into contact with the embryo.

Up until the moment when the screen had come alive with the image, the pregnancy had been an abstract thing to Jake. Even—if he were to be really honest with himself—an *inconvenient* thing. But there on the screen had appeared a *baby*. Only about six centimetres at this stage, the radiographer had explained, but a totally recognisable baby. With hands and feet and a *face*.

To the palpable relief of everyone in the room, a strong and steady amplified heartbeat had been clearly audible. The baby had been moving around and show-ing no signs of being affected by Eliza's inability to keep down so very little food over the last weeks. It had looked as if it was having a ball, floating in the amniotic fluid, secure in Eliza's womb.

Jake had felt as if his heart had stopped beating, and his lungs had gone into arrest as, mesmerised, he'd watched that image. He was a man who never cried but he'd felt tears of awe and amazement threatening to betray him. He hadn't been able to look at Eliza—the sheer joy shining from her face would have tipped him over. Without seeming to be aware she was doing it, she had reached for his hand and gripped it hard. All he'd been able to do was squeeze it back.

This was a real baby. A child. A *person*. Against all odds he and Eliza had created a new life.

What he had to do had become very clear.

CHAPTER TWELVE

THE NEXT DAY Eliza was surprised at how weak she still felt as Jake helped her up the narrow, steep stairs to her bedroom in the converted attic of her house. She usually bounded up them.

'Just lean on me,' he said.

'I don't want to lean on anyone,' she said, more crossly than she had intended.

Forcing herself to keep her distance from this gorgeous man was stressful. Even feeling weak and fatigued, she still fancied him like crazy. But way back in Port Douglas she'd already decided that wasn't enough. Just because she was pregnant it didn't change things.

'Sometimes you have to, Eliza.'

She knew he wasn't only referring to her taking the physical support his broad shoulders offered.

'You can't get through this on your own.'

There was an edge of impatience to his voice she hadn't heard before. Looking after her the way he'd done yesterday, and now today, wasn't part of their four-day fling agreement. That had been about uncomplicated fun and uninhibited sex. Now he must feel he was stuck with her when she was unwell. He couldn't be more wrong. She didn't need his help.

'I appreciate your concern, truly I do,' she said. 'You've been so good to me. But I'm not on my own. I have friends. My GP is only a block away. I spoke to her yesterday after you left the hospital. Both she and the practice nurse can make home visits if required.'

'You need to be looked after,' he said stubbornly.

Eliza's heart sank as she foresaw them clashing over this. She had been perturbed at how Jake had taken over her vacation—how much more perturbing was the thought that he might take over her life?

Eliza reached the top of the stairs. Took the few steps required to take her to her bed and sat down on the edge with a sigh of relief.

'I'd prefer to look after myself,' she said. 'I'm quite capable of it, you know.'

'It didn't look that way to me yesterday.' He swore under his breath. 'Eliza, what might have happened if I hadn't got here when I did? What if you'd passed out on the bathroom floor? Hit your head on the way down?'

She paused for a long moment. 'It's a very scary thought. I will never be able to thank you enough for being there for me, Jake. Why *did* you come to my house when you did?'

'The obvious. I didn't get why you blanked me at the party and I wanted an explanation.'

Her chin lifted. 'Why did you feel you were owed an explanation? We had a fling. I didn't want to pick up from where we left off. Enough said.'

'Now you're pregnant. That makes it very different. From where I stand, it doesn't seem like you're doing a very good job of looking after yourself.'

Her hackles rose. 'This is all very new to me. It's a steep learning curve.' Eliza took a deep, calming breath. She couldn't let herself get too defensive. Not when Jake had pretty much had to pick her up from the floor.

'There's a lot at stake if you don't learn more quickly,' he said.

She gritted her teeth. 'Don't you think I *know* that? While I was lying there in that hospital bed I kept wondering how I had let myself get into that state.'

'I suspect you thought the sickness was a natural part of pregnancy. That you had to put up with the nausea. Perhaps if you'd told your friends you were pregnant they might have seen what you were going through wasn't normal and that you were headed into a danger zone.'

Eliza wasn't sure whether he was being sympathetic or delivering a reprimand. 'When did you get to know so much?' she said, deciding to err on the side of offered sympathy. The direction of where this conversation was beginning to go scared her. It almost sounded as though it might lead into an accusation that she was an incompetent mother—before she'd even give birth.

'Since yesterday, when the hospital doctor explained it,' he said with a shrug of his broad shoulders. 'I learned more than I ever thought I'd need to know about that particular complication.'

How many men would have just dropped her at the hospital and run? She was grateful to Jake—but she did *not* want him to take over.

'I've learned a lot too,' she said. 'If I keep on top of the nausea, and don't let myself get dehydrated, that shouldn't happen again. I admit this has given me a real shock. I had no reason to think I wouldn't fly through pregnancy with my usual good health. But the doctors have given me strategies to deal with it. Including more time in the hospital on a drip if required. I'll be okay.'

He shook his head. 'I wish I could believe that. But I suspect you'll be back at Party Queens, dragging a drip on its stand along behind you, before you know it.'

That forced a reluctant smile from her. But he wasn't smiling and her smile quickly faded. He was spot-on in his assessment of her workaholic tendencies. Though she didn't appreciate his lack of faith in her ability to look after herself.

'Jake, trust me—I won't over-extend myself. Miracles don't come along too often in a person's life.' She placed her hand protectively on her bump. 'Truth is, this is almost certainly my only chance to have a baby. I won't jeopardise anything by being foolish. Believe me—if I need help, I'll ask for it.'

Asking for help didn't come easily to her. Because with accepting help came loss of control. One of her biggest issues in management training had been learning to delegate. Now it looked as if she might have to learn to give over a degree of control in her private life too. To doctors, nurses, other health professionals. Because she had to consider her baby as well as herself. But she would not give control over to a man.

For a converted attic in a small house, the bedroom was spacious, with an en suite shower room and a study nook as well as sleeping quarters. But Jake was so tall, so broad-shouldered, he made the space seem suddenly cramped.

How she wished things could be different. Despite all that had happened desire shimmered through her when she feasted her eyes on him, impossibly handsome in black jeans and a black T-shirt. Jake, here in her bedroom, was looking totally smokin'.

Then there was her—with lank hair, yesterday's clothes, a big wad of sterile gauze taped to the back of her hand where the drip had been, and a plastic hospital ID band still around her wrist. Oh, and pregnant.

Jake paced the length of the room and back several times, to the point when Eliza started to get nervous without really knowing why. He stood in front of the window for a long moment with his back to her. Then pivoted on his heel to turn back to face her.

'We have to get married,' he said, without preamble.

Eliza's mouth went dry and her heart started to thud. She was so shocked all she could do was stare up at him. '*What?*' she finally managed to choke out. 'Where did *that* come from?' She pulled herself up from the bed to face him, though her shaky knees told her she really should stay seated.

'You're pregnant. It's the right thing to do.'

He looked over her head rather than directly at her. There was no light in his eyes, no anticipation—nothing of the expression she might expect from a man proposing marriage.

'Get married because I'm pregnant?'

She knew she was just repeating his statement but she needed time to think.

'We have to get married,' he'd commanded. There had been no joy, no feeling, certainly no talk of love—and that hurt more than it should have. Not that *love* had ever come into their relationship. Worse, there had been no consultation with her. She'd rank it more as a demand than a proposal. And demands didn't sit well with her.

What would she have done if he had actually proposed? With words of affection and hope? She couldn't think about that. That had never been part of their agreement.

'You being pregnant is reason enough,' he said.

'No, it isn't. You know I don't want to marry again. Even if I did, we don't know each other well enough to consider such a big step.'

The irony of it didn't escape her. They knew each other well enough to make a baby. Not well enough to spend their lives together.

She shook her head. 'I can't do it, Jake.'

The first time she'd married for love—or what she'd thought was love—and it had been a disaster. Why would marrying for less than love be any better? Marrying someone she'd known for such a short time? An even shorter time than she'd known her ex.

'Your pregnancy changes everything,' Jake said. His face was set in severe lines.

'It does. But not in that way.'

'You're having a baby. *My* baby. I want to marry you.'

'Why? For my reputation? Because of the media?'

There was a long pause before he spoke. 'To give the baby a father,' he said. 'The baby deserves to have two parents.'

That was the last reason she would have anticipated from him and it took her aback for a moment. She put her hand to her heart to try and slow its sudden racing. 'Jake, that's honourable of you. But it's not necessary for you to marry me. If you want to be involved with the baby I'm happy—'

'I want the baby to have my name,' he said. 'And a good life.'

'*I* can give him or her a good life. You don't have to do this. We knew marriage wasn't an option for us.'

'It's important to me, Eliza.'

She noticed his fists, clenched by his sides. The tension in his voice. There was something more here—something that belied the straightforwardness of his words.

'You married your ex-wife because she was pregnant,' she said. 'I don't expect that. Really I don't. Please stop pacing the room like a caged lion.'

Her knees felt suddenly too weak to support her. She wanted to collapse back onto the bed. Instead she sat down slowly, controlled, suddenly fearing to show any weakness. Jake was a man used to getting what he wanted. Now it seemed he wanted *her*. Correction. He wanted her for the baby she was carrying. *His baby.*

'Why, Jake? You said you never wanted to be a father. Why this sudden interest?'

Jake sat down on the bed beside her, as far away from her as he could without colliding with the bedhead. He braced both hands on his knees. Overlying Eliza's nervousness was a pang of mingled longing and regret. Back in Port Douglas they wouldn't have been sitting side by side on a bed, being careful not to touch. They would have been making love by now, lost in a breathtaking world of intimacy and mutual pleasure. *Lovemaking that had created a miracle baby.*

'Seeing the baby on the ultrasound affected me yesterday,' he said now. 'The pregnancy which, up until then had been an abstract thing, became very real for me.'

Eliza noticed how weary he looked, with shadows

under his eyes, lines she hadn't noticed before etched by his mouth. She wondered how much sleep he'd had last night. Had he been awake half the night, wrangling with the dilemma she had presented him with by unexpectedly bearing his baby?

'It affected me too.'

She remembered she had been so overcome that she had gripped his hand—so tightly it must have hurt him. Then she had intercepted a smiling glance from the nurse. She and Jake must have looked quite the proud parents-to-be. If only that sweet nurse had known the less than romantic truth.

'You didn't see a scan when your ex—Fern—was pregnant?' she asked Jake.

'She didn't believe in medical intervention of any kind.'

'But an ultrasound isn't like an X-ray. It's safe and—'

'I know that. But that's beside the point. The point is I saw a little person yesterday. A tiny baby who is going to grow up to be a boy, like I was, or a girl like you were. We didn't plan it. We didn't want—'

She put up a hand in a halt sign, noticed her hand wasn't quite steady. 'Stop right there. You mightn't want it—I mean him or her... I hate calling my baby "it"—but I *do* want him or her. Very much.'

'I'm aware of how much you want the baby. Of the tragedy it was for you to discover you couldn't conceive. But the fact is I didn't want children. I would never have chosen to embark on a pregnancy with you. You know that.'

His words stung. Not just because of his rejection of her but because of her baby, unwanted by its father. No

way would she have chosen a man she scarcely knew—
a man who didn't want kids—as the father of her baby.

'I know we had a deal for four days of no-strings
fun,' she said. 'Mother Nature had other ideas. Trust
me—I wouldn't have *chosen* to have a child this way
either.'

He indicated her bump. 'This is no longer just about
me or about you; it's about another person at the start
of life. And it's *my* responsibility. This child deserves
a better life than you can give it on your own.'

If that wasn't an insult from an arrogant billionaire,
she didn't know what was.

She forced herself to sound calm and reasonable.
'Jake, I might not be as wealthy as you, but I can give
my child a more than decent life, thank you very much.
I'm hardly a pauper.'

'Don't delude yourself, Eliza. You can't give it anything *like* what I have the resources to provide.'

Perspiration beaded on her forehead and she had to
clasp her hands to stop them from trembling. It wasn't
just that she was still feeling weak. She had a sudden,
horrible premonition that she was preparing to do battle for her own child.

So quickly this had turned adversarial. From a proposal to a stand-off. She couldn't help but think how
different this would be if she and Jake were together on
this. As together and in tune as they had been in bed.
Instead they were sitting here, apart on the bed, glar-
ing at each other—she the mother, he the inadvertent
sperm donor who wanted to take things further than
he had any right to do.

'I can—and will—give this child a good life on

my own,' she said. 'He or she will have everything they need.'

Jake was so wealthy. He could buy anything he wanted. What was he capable of doing if he wanted to take her child from her?

'Except its father's name,' he said.

Eliza was taken aback. She'd expected him to talk about private schooling, a mansion, travel, the best of everything as far as material goods went. Not the one intangible thing she could not provide.

'Is *that* what this is about?' she said. 'Some patriarchal thing?'

'What is that meant to mean?' He stared at her as if she'd suddenly sprouted horns. 'This is about making my child legitimate. Giving it its rightful place in the world.'

My child. How quickly he had claimed her baby as his own.

'Legitimate? What does *that* mean these days?' she asked.

He gave a short, sharp bark of laughter she'd never heard from him before. 'I went through hell as a kid because I was illegitimate. Life for a boy with no father was no fun at all.' His mouth set in a grim line.

'That was thirty years ago, Jake,' she said, trying not to sound combative about an issue that was obviously sensitive for him. 'Attitudes have changed now.'

'Have they really? I wonder... I walked the walk. Not just the bullying from the kids, but the sneering from the adults towards my mother, the insensitivity of the schoolteachers. Father's Day at school was the worst day of the year. The kids all making cards and gifts for their dads... Me with no one. I don't want to risk putting my child through what I went through.'

He traced the slight crookedness of his nose with his index finger. The imperfection only made him more handsome, Eliza had always thought.

'Surely it wasn't such a stigma then?' she asked.

He scowled. 'You have no idea, do you?' he said. 'Born into a family with a father who provided for you. Who gave you his name. His protection.'

Eliza felt this was spiralling away from her. Into something so much deeper than she'd realised. 'No, I don't. Have any idea, I mean.'

One of her first memories was of her father lifting her for the first time up onto a horse's back, with big, gentle hands. How proud he'd been of her fearlessness. No matter what had come afterwards, she had that. Other scenes of her father and her with their beloved horses jostled against the edges of her memory.

Jake's face was set into such grim lines he almost looked ugly. 'Every time I got called the B-word I had to answer the insult with my fists. My mother cried the first time I came home with a broken nose. She soon ran out of tears. Until the day I got big enough to deliver some broken noses of my own.'

Eliza shuddered at the aggression in his voice, but at the same time her heart went out to that little boy. 'I didn't realise how bad it was not to have a dad at home.'

'It's a huge, aching gap.'

His green eyes were clouded with a sadness that tore at her.

'Not one I want my own child to fall into.'

'Why wasn't your father around?'

'Because he was a selfish pig of a man who denied my existence. Is that a good enough answer?'

The bitterness in his voice shocked Eliza. She imagined a dear little boy, with a shock of blond hair and green eyes, suffering a pain more intense than that of any broken nose. She yearned to comfort him but didn't know what she could say about such a deep-seated hurt. At the same time she had to hold back on her feelings of sympathy when it came to Jake. She had to be on top of her game if Jake was going to get tough.

He sighed. Possibly he didn't realise the depth of anguish in that sigh.

She couldn't stop herself from placing her hand over his. 'I'm sorry, Jake. It was his loss.'

He nodded a silent acknowledgment.

Back in Port Douglas she had yearned for Jake to share his deeper side with her. Now she'd been tossed into its dark depths and she felt she was drowning in a sea of hurts and secrets, pulled every which way by conflicting currents. On top of her nausea, and her worries about handling life as a single mother, she wasn't sure she had the emotional fortitude to deal with this.

'Do you know anything about your father?'

About the man who was, she realised with a shock, her unborn child's grandfather. Jake's mother would be his or her grandmother. Through their son or daughter she and Jake would be connected for the rest of their lives—whether they wanted to be or not.

'It's a short, ugly story,' he said, his mouth a grim line. 'My mother was a trainee nurse at a big Brisbane training hospital. She was very pretty and very naïve. He was a brilliant, handsome doctor and she fell for him. She didn't know he was engaged to a girl from a wealthy family. He seduced her. She fell pregnant. He didn't want to know about it. She got booted out of her job in disgrace and slunk home to her parents at the Gold Coast.'

The father handsome, the mother pretty... Both obviously intelligent... For the first time a thought flashed through Eliza's head. Would the baby look like her or like Jake? Be as smart? It wasn't speculation she felt she could share with him.

'That's the end of it?' she said. 'What about child support?'

'Not a cent. He was tricky. My mother's family couldn't afford lawyers. She wanted nothing to do with him. Just to get on with her life. My grandparents helped raise me, though they didn't have much. It was a struggle.'

Poor little Jake. Imagine growing up with *that* as his heritage. Before the drought her parents had loved to tell the story of how they had met at an agricultural show—her dad competing in the Western riding, her mum winning ribbons for her scones and fruitcake. She wondered if they remembered it now. Would her child want to know how she and his or her dad had met? How would she explain why they weren't together?

'You never met him?' she asked.

'As a child, no.' Jake's mouth curled with contempt. 'But when media reports started appearing on the "young genius" who'd become a billionaire, he came sniffing around, looking for his long-lost son.'

'What did you do?'

'Kicked him to the kerb—like he'd sent my mother packing.'

Eliza shuddered at the strength of vengeful satisfaction in his voice. Jake would make a formidable enemy if crossed.

Jake got up from the bed. It was hard to think straight, sitting so close to Eliza She looked so wan and frail, somehow even more beautiful. Her usual sweet, floral scent had a sharp overtone of hospital from the bandage on her hand, which reminded him of what she had been through. He would never forget that terrifying moment when he'd thought she had stopped breathing.

He fought a powerful impulse to fold her in his arms and hold her close. She needed him, and yet he couldn't seem to make her see that. He wanted to look after her. Make sure she and the baby had everything they needed. If his own father had looked after his mother the way he wanted to look after Eliza, how different his life might have been. Yet he sensed a battle on his hands even to get access to his child.

He hadn't intended to confide in her about his father. Next thing he'd be spilling the details of his criminal record. Of his darkest day of despair when he'd thought he couldn't endure another minute of his crappy life. But he'd hoped telling her something of his past might make her more amenable to the idea of getting married to give their child a name.

'I'm asking you again to marry me, Eliza. Before the baby is born. So it—'

'Can you please not call the baby *it*? Try *he* or *she*. This is a little person we're talking about here. I thought you got that?'

He felt safer calling the baby *it*. Calling it *he* or *she* made it seem too real. And the more real it seemed, the more he would get attached. And he couldn't let himself get too attached if Eliza was going to keep the baby from him.

He didn't know a lot about custody arrangements for a child with single parents—though he suspected he was soon to know a whole lot more. But he doubted the courts were much inclined to give custody of a newborn to anyone other than its mother. No matter how much money he threw at the best possible legal representation. Once it got a little older that would be a different matter. His child would not grow up without a father the way he had.

'I want you to marry me before the baby is born so *he* or *she* is legitimate,' he said.

She glared at him. 'Jake, I've told you I don't want to get married. To you or to anyone else. And if I did it would be because I was in love with my husband-to-be.'

Jake gritted his teeth. He had married before for love and look where it had got him. 'That sounds very idealistic, Eliza. But there can be pragmatic reasons to marry, too. There have been throughout history. To secure alliances or fortunes. Or to gain property or close a business deal. Or to legitimise a child.'

Slowly she shook her head. A lock of her hair fell across her eyes. She needed a haircut. She'd obviously been neglecting herself. Why couldn't she see that she needed someone to look after her? *Vulnerable.* That was what Andie had called her. Yet Eliza just didn't seem to see it.

Her eyes narrowed. 'I wish you could hear how you sound, Jake. Cold. Ruthless. This isn't a business deal we're brokering. It's our lives. You. Me. A loveless marriage.'

'A way to ensure our child is legitimate.'

'What about a way to have a woman squirming under a man's thumb? That was *my* experience of marriage. And I have no desire to experience it again.'

'Really?' he said. 'I wouldn't want to see you squirming. Or under my thumb.' Jake held up his fingers in a fist, his thumb to the side. 'See? It's not nearly large enough to hold you down.'

It was a feeble attempt at levity and he knew it. But this was the most difficult conversation he had ever had. The stakes were so much higher than in even the most lucrative of potential business deals.

'I don't know whether to take that as an insult or not. I'm not *that* big.'

'No, you're not. In fact you're not big enough. You've lost weight, Eliza. You need to gain it. I can look after you as well as the baby.'

Her chin lifted in the stubborn way he was beginning to recognise.

'I don't *want* to be looked after. I can look after both myself and my baby on my own. You can see him or her, play a role in their life. But I most certainly don't want to *marry* you.'

'You're making a mistake, Eliza. Are you sure you don't want to reconsider?'

'You can't force me to marry you, Jake.'

'But I can make life so much easier for you if you do,' he said.

'Love is the only reason to marry. But love hasn't entered the equation for us. For that reason alone, I can't marry you.'

'That's your final word?'

She nodded.

He got up. 'Then you'll be hearing from my lawyer.'

Eliza's already pale face drained of every remaining scrap of colour. *'What?'*

She leapt up from the bed, had to steady herself as she seemed to rock on her feet as if she were dizzy. But she pushed aside his steadying hand and glared at him.

'You heard me,' he said. 'I intend to seek custody.'

'You can't have custody over an unborn child.' Her voice was high and strained.

'You're about to see what I can do,' he said.

He turned on his heel, strode to the top of the stairs. Flimsy stairs. Too dangerous. She couldn't bring up a child in this house. He ignored the inner voice that told him this house was a hundred times safer and nicer than the welfare housing apartment he'd grown up in. *Nothing but the best for his child.*

She put up her hand in a feeble attempt to stop him. 'Jake. You can't go.'

'I'm gone, Eliza. I suggest you get back to bed and rest. An agency nurse will be arriving in an hour. I've employed her to look after you for the next three days, as per doctor's orders. I suggest you let her in and allow her to care for you. Otherwise you might end up back in hospital.'

He swung himself on to the top step.

'I'll see you in court.'

CHAPTER THIRTEEN

SO IT HAD come to this. Eliza placed her hand protectively on her bump as she rode the elevator up to the twenty-third floor of the prestigious building in the heart of the central business district of Sydney, where the best law firms had their offices. She hadn't heard from Jake for three weeks. All communication had been through their lawyers. Except for one challenging email.

Now she was headed to a meeting with Jake and his lawyers to finalise a legal document that spelled out in detail a custody and support agreement for the unborn Baby Dunne.

She must have paled at the thought of the confrontation to come, because her lawyer gave her arm a squeeze of support. Jake had, of course, engaged the most expensive and well-known family law attorney in Sydney to be on his side of the battle lines.

He'd sent her an email.

Are you sure you can afford not to marry me, Eliza? Just your lawyer's fees alone will stop you in your tracks.

What he didn't realise, high up there in his billionaire world, where the almighty dollar ruled, was that not everybody could be bought. She had an older cousin who was a brilliant family lawyer. And Cousin Maree was so outraged at what Jake was doing that she was representing Eliza *pro bono*. Well, not quite for free. Eliza had agreed that Party Queens would organise the most spectacular twenty-first birthday party possible for Maree's daughter.

Now, Maree squeezed her arm reassuringly. 'Chin up. Just let me do the talking, okay?'

Eliza nodded, rather too numbed at the thought of what she was about to face to do anything else *but* keep quiet.

She saw Jake the moment she entered the large, traditionally furnished meeting room. Her heart gave such a jolt she had to hold on for support to the back of one of the chairs that were ranged around the boardroom table. He was standing tall, in front of floor-to-ceiling windows that looked out on a magnificent mid-morning view of Sydney Harbour. The Bridge loomed so closely she felt she could reach out and touch it.

Jake was wearing a deep charcoal-grey business suit, immaculately tailored to his broad shoulders and tapered to his waist. His hair—darker now, less sun-streaked—crept over his collar. No angel wings in sight—rather the forked tail and dark horns of the demon who had tormented her for the last three weeks with his demands.

At the sound of her entering the room Jake turned. For a split second his gaze met hers. There was a flash of recognition—and something else that was gone so soon she scarcely registered it. But it could have been regret. Then the shutters came down to blank his expression.

'Eliza,' he said curtly, acknowledging her presence with a brief nod in her direction.

'Jake,' she said coolly, despite her inner turmoil.

Her brain, so firmly in charge up until now, had been once more vanquished by her libido—she refused to entertain for even one second the thought that it might be her heart—which flamed into life at the sight of the beautiful man who had been her lover for those four, glorious days. So treacherous her libido, still to clamour for this man. Her lover who had become her enemy—the hero of her personal fairytale transformed into the villain.

Eliza let Jake's lawyer's assistant pull out the chair for her. Before she sat she straightened her shoulders and stood proud. Her tailored navy dress with its large white collar was tucked and pleated to accommodate and show off her growing bump. She hoped her silent message was loud and clear—*she* was in possession of the prize.

But at the same time as she displayed the ace in her hand she felt swept by a wave of inexplicable longing for Jake to be sharing the milestones of her pregnancy with her. She hadn't counted on the loneliness factor of single motherhood. There was a vague bubbling sensation that meant the baby was starting to kick, she thought. At fifteen weeks it was too soon for her to be feeling vigorous activity; she knew that from the 'what to expect' pregnancy books and websites she read obsessively. But she had a sudden vision of Jake, resting his hand on her tummy, a look of expectant joy on his face as he waited to feel the kicking of their baby's tiny feet.

That could only happen in a parallel universe. Jake had no interest in her other than as an incubator.

She wondered, too, if he had really thought ahead to his interaction with their son or daughter? His motivation seemed purely to be making up for the childhood he felt he'd lost because of his own despicable father. To try to right a family wrong and force a certain lifestyle on her whether she liked it or not.

What if their child—who might be equally as smart and stubborn as his or her parents—had other ideas about how he or she wanted to live? He or she might be as fiercely independent as both her, Eliza, and the paternal grandmother—Jake's mother.

Would she ever get to meet his mother? Unlikely. Unless she was there when Eliza handed over their child for Jake's court-prescribed visits.

That was not how it was meant to be. She ached at the utter *wrongness* of this whole arrangement.

Jake settled in to a chair directly opposite her, his lawyer to his right. That was *his* silent statement, she supposed. Confrontation, with the battlefield between them. *Bring it on,* she thought.

It was fortunate that the highly polished dark wooden table was wide enough so there was no chance of his knees nudging hers, her foot brushing against his when she shifted in her seat. Because, despite all the hostility, her darn libido still longed for his touch. It was insane—and must surely be blamed on the up-and-down hormone fluctuations of pregnancy.

Maree cleared her throat. 'Shall we start the proceedings? This is very straightforward.'

Maree had explained all this to her before, but Eliza listened intently as her cousin spoke, at the same time keeping her gaze firmly fixed on Jake's face. He gave nothing away—not the merest flicker of reaction. He ran his finger along his collar and tugged at his tie— obviously uncomfortable at being 'trussed up'. But she guessed he'd wanted to look like an intimidating billionaire businessman in front of the lawyers.

Maree explained how legally there could not be any formal custody proceedings over an unborn child. However, the parties had agreed to prepare a document outlining joint custody to present to a judge after the event of a live birth.

Eliza had known that particular phrase would be coming and bit her lip hard. She caught Jake's eye, and his slight nod indicated his understanding of how difficult it was for her to hear it. Because its implication was that something could go wrong in the meantime. Her greatest fear was that she would lose this miracle baby—although her doctor had assured her the pregnancy was progressing very well.

Jake's hands were gripped so tightly together that his knuckles showed white—perhaps he feared it too. He had been so brilliant that day he'd taken her to hospital.

Eliza was looking for crumbs to indicate that Jake wasn't the enemy, that this was all a big misunderstanding. That brief show of empathy from him might be it. Then she remembered why she was here in the first place. To be coerced into signing an agreement she didn't want to sign.

She was being held to a threat—hinted at rather than spoken out in the open—that if she didn't cooperate Jake would use his influence to steer wealthy clients away from Party Queens. Right at a time when her ongoing intermittent nausea and time away from work, plus the departure of their new head chef to a rival firm, meant her beloved company—and her livelihood—was tipping towards a precipice. What choice did she have?

Maree continued in measured tones, saying that both parties acknowledged Jake Marlowe's paternity, so there would be no need for a court-ordered genetic test once the baby was born. She listed the terms of the proposed custody agreement, starting with limited visits by the father while the child was an infant, progressing to full-on division of weekends and vacations. The baby's legal name would be Baby Dunne-Marlowe—once the sex was known a first name satisfactory to both parents would be agreed upon.

Then Jake's lawyer took over, listing the generous support package to be provided by Mr Marlowe—all medical expenses paid, a house to be gifted in the child's name and held in trust by Mr Marlowe, a trust fund to be set up for—

Eliza half got up from her chair. She couldn't endure this sham a second longer. 'That's enough. I know what's in the document. Just give it to me and I'll sign.'

She subsided in her chair. Bent her head to take Maree's counsel.

'Are you sure?' her cousin asked in a low voice. 'You don't want further clarification of the trust fund provisions? Or the—?'

'No. I just want this to be over.'

The irony of it struck her. Jake had been worried about gold-diggers. Now he was insisting she receive money she didn't want, binding her with ties that were choking all the joyful anticipation of her pregnancy. She tried to focus on the baby. That precious little person growing safe and happy inside her. Her unborn child was all that mattered.

She avoided looking at Jake as she signed everywhere the multiple-paged document indicated her signature was required, stabbing the pen so hard the paper tore.

Jake followed Eliza as she departed the conference room, apparently so eager to get away from him that she'd broken into a half-run. She was almost to the bank of elevators, her low-heeled shoes tapping on the marble floor, before he caught up with her.

'Eliza,' he called.

SHe didn't turn around, but he was close enough to hear her every word.

'I have nothing to say to you, Jake. You've got what you wanted, so just go away.'

Only she didn't say *go away*. She used far pithier language.

She reached the elevator and jabbed the elevator button. Once, twice, then kept on jabbing it.

'That won't get it here any faster,' he said, and immediately regretted the words. *Why had he said something so condescending?* He cursed his inability to find the right words in moments of high tension and emotion.

She turned on him, blue eyes flashing the brightest he'd seen them. Bright with threatening tears, he realised. Tears of anger—directed at *him*.

'Of course it won't. But I live in hope. Because the sooner I can get away from you, the better. Even a second or two would help.' She went back to jabbing the button.

Her baby bump had grown considerably since he'd last seen her. She looked the picture of an elegant, perfectly groomed businesswoman. The smart, feisty Eliza he had come to— Come to what? Respect? Admire? Something more than that. Something, despite all they'd gone through, he couldn't put a name to.

'You look well,' he said. *She looked more beautiful than ever.*

With a sigh of frustration she dropped her finger from the elevator button. Aimed a light kick at the elevator door. She turned to face him, her eyes narrowed with hostility.

'Don't try and engage me in polite chit-chat. Just because you've forced me to sign a proposed custody agreement it doesn't mean you own me—like you're trying to own my baby.'

You didn't own children—and you couldn't force a woman to marry you. Belatedly he'd come to that realisation.

Jake didn't often admit to feeling ashamed. But shame was what had overwhelmed him during the meeting, as he'd watched the emotions flickering over Eliza's face, so easy to read.

He'd been a teenage troublemaker—the leader of a group of other angry, alienated kids like himself. Taller and more powerful than the others, he'd used his off-the-charts IQ and well-developed street-smarts to control and intimidate the gang—even those older than him.

He'd thought he'd put all that long behind him. Then in that room, sitting opposite Eliza—proud, brave Eliza—it had struck him in the gut like a physical blow. He'd behaved as badly towards her as he had in his worst days as a teenage gang leader. Jim Hill would be ashamed of him—but not as ashamed as he was of himself.

'I'm sorry, Eliza. I didn't mean it to go this far.'

She blinked away the threatening tears. 'You played dirty, Jake. I wouldn't marry you, so you brought in the big guns. I would have played fair with you. Visitation rights. Even the Dunne-Marlowe name. For the sake of our baby. I was *glad* you wanted to play a role in our child's life. But I wasn't in a space for making life-changing decisions right then. I'd just got out of hospital.'

How had he let this get so far? 'I was wrong. I should have—'

'Now the document is signed you think you can placate me? Forget it. Don't you see? You're so concerned about giving this child your name, you're bequeathing to him or her something much worse. A mother who resents her baby's father. Who hates him for the way she's had to fight against him imposing his will on her, riding roughshod over her feelings.'

Now he was on the ground, being kicked from all sides. And the blows were much harder than those Eliza had given the elevator door.

'*Hate?* That's a strong word.'

'Not strong enough for how I feel about you,' she said, tight-lipped. 'I reckon you've let the desire to win overcome all your common sense and feelings of decency.'

Of course. He'd been guilty of *over-thinking* on a grand scale. 'I just want to do the right thing by our child,' he said. 'To look after it and to look after you too, Eliza. You need me.'

She shook her head. 'I don't need you. At one stage I wanted you. And…and I… I could have cared for you. When you danced me around that ballroom in Montovia I thought I was on the brink of something momentous in my life.'

'So did I,' he said slowly.

'Then there was Port Douglas. Leaving you seemed so *wrong*. We had something *real*. Only we were so darn intent on protecting ourselves from hurt we didn't recognise it and we walked away from it. The baby gave us a second chance. To be friends. Maybe more than friends. But we blew that too.'

'There must be such a thing as a third chance,' he said.

She shook her head so vehemently it dislodged the clip that was holding her hair off her face and she had to push it back into place with hands that trembled.

'No more chances. Not after what happened in that room today. You won't break me. I will never forgive you. For the baby's sake, I'll be civil. It would be wrong to pump our child's mind with poison against his or her father. Even if I happen to think he's a…a bullying thug.' Her cheeks were flushed scarlet, her eyes glittered.

Now he'd been kicked to a pulp—bruised black and blue all over. Hadn't the judge used a similar expression when sentencing him to juvenile detention? The words *bully* and *thug* seemed to be familiar. But that had been so long ago. He'd been fifteen years of age. Why had those tendencies he'd thought left well and truly behind him in adolescence surfaced again?

Then it hit him—the one final blow he hadn't seen coming. It came swinging again like that sledgehammer from nowhere to slam him in the head. This wasn't about Eliza needing him—it was about *him* needing *her*. Needing her so desperately he'd gone to crazy lengths to try to secure her.

Just then the elevator arrived.

'At last,' Eliza said as she stepped towards it. She had to wait until a girl clutching a bunch of legal folders to her chest stepped out.

'Eliza.'

Jake went to catch her arm, to stop her leaving. There was so much he had to say to her, to explain. But she shrugged off his hand.

'Please, Jake, no more. I can't take it. I'll let you know when the baby is born. As per our contract.'

She stood facing him as the elevator doors started to slide slowly inward. The last thing he saw of her was a slice of her face, with just one fat, glistening tear sliding down her cheek.

Jake stood for a long time, watching the indicator marking the elevator's progress down the twenty-three floors. He felt frozen to that marble floor, unable to step backwards or forwards.

When the elevator reached the ground floor he turned on his heel and strode back to his meeting. He needed to rethink his strategy. Jake Marlowe was not a man who gave up easily.

CHAPTER FOURTEEN

THE LAST PLACE Eliza expected to be a week after the lawyers' meeting with Jake was on an executive jet flying to Europe. Despite the gravity of the reason for her flight, it was a welcome distraction.

Gemma had called an emergency meeting of the three Party Queens directors. Eliza's unexpected pregnancy had tipped the problem of an absentee director into crisis point. And because Gemma was Crown Princess, as well as their Food Director, she had sent the Montovian royal family's private jet to transport Eliza and Andie from Sydney to Montovia for the meeting.

Just because Gemma *could*, Eliza had mused with a smile when she'd got the summons, along with the instructions for when a limousine would pick her up to take her to the airport where she would meet Andie.

Dominic had decided to come along for the flight, too. He and Andie's little boy Hugo was being looked after by his doting grandma and grandpa—Andie's parents.

Eliza was very fond of Andie's husband. But despite the luxury of the flight—the lounge chair comfort of leather upholstery, the crystal etched with the Monto-

vian royal coat of arms, the restaurant-quality food, the
hotel-style bathrooms—she hadn't been able to relax
because of the vaguely hostile emanations coming her
way from Dominic.

Jake was Dominic's best male friend. The bonds between them went deep. According to the legend of the
two young billionaires they went way back, to when
they'd been in their first year at university. Together,
they had built fortunes. Created a charitable foundation
for homeless kids. And cemented that young friendship into something adult and enduring.

In the air, somewhere over Indonesia, Dominic told
Eliza in no uncertain terms that Jake was unhappy and
miserable. He couldn't understand why Eliza wouldn't
just marry Jake and put them *all* out of their misery.

Dominic got a sharp poke in the ribs from his wife's
elbow for *that* particular opinion. He was referring to
the fact that sympathies had been split down the mid-
dle among the other two Party Queens and their re-
spective spouses.

Andie and Gemma were on her side—though they'd
been at pains to state that they weren't actually *taking* sides. Neither of her friends saw why Eliza should
marry a man she didn't love just to give her baby Jake's
name when he or she was born. Nor did they approve of
the domineering way Jake had tried to force the issue.

Dominic and Tristan, however, thought differently.

Dominic had an abusive childhood behind him—
tough times living on the streets. He'd told Eliza she
was both crazy and unwise not to jump straight into
the safety net Jake was offering.

Tristan, a hereditary Crown Prince, also couldn't

see the big deal. There was only one way forward. The baby carried Jake's blood. As far as Tristan was concerned, Gemma had told Eliza, Jake was doing the correct and honourable thing in offering Eliza marriage. Eliza must do the right thing and accept. That from a man who had changed the laws of his country regarding marriage so he could marry for love and make Gemma his wife.

Both men had let Eliza know that they saw her stance as stubborn in the extreme, and contributing to an unnecessary rift between very close friends. They stood one hundred per cent by their generous and maligned buddy Jake. The women could not believe how blindly loyal their husbands were to the *bullying thug* that was Jake.

Of course Eliza was well aware that neither Andie nor Gemma had ever called Jake that in front of Dominic or Tristan. They were each way too wise to let problems with their mutual friends interfere with their own blissfully happy marriages to the men they adored. Besides, as Andie told Eliza, they actually still liked Jake a lot. They just didn't like the way he'd treated her.

'Although Jake *is* very generous,' Andie reminded her.

'Of course he is—exceedingly generous,' said Eliza evenly.

Inside she was screaming: *And sexy and kind and even funny when he wants to be.* As if she needed to be reminded of his good points when they were all she seemed to think about these days.

She kept remembering that time in the ambulance, as she'd drifted in and out of consciousness and the man who had never let go of her hand had murmured reassurance and encouragement all the way to the hospital. The man who'd chartered a private boat for her because she'd said she wanted to dive on the Great Barrier Reef. The man who hadn't needed angel wings to send her soaring to heaven when they'd made love.

Eliza wished, not for the first time, that she hadn't actually called Jake a bullying thug—or told Andie she'd called him that. That day she'd got all the way to the bottom of the building on the elevator and seriously considered going all the way back up to apologise. Then realised, as she had just told him she hated him, that it might not be the best of ideas.

'Do you ever regret not marrying him?' Andie asked. 'You would never have to worry about money again.'

'No,' Eliza replied firmly. 'Because I don't think financial security is a good enough reason to marry—not for me, anyway. Not when I'm confident I'll always be able to earn a good living.'

What she couldn't admit—not even to her dearest friend Andie, and certainly not to Dominic—was that these weeks away from Jake had made her realise how much she had grown to care for him. That along with all the other valid reasons for her not to marry Jake there was one overwhelming reason—she couldn't put herself through the torture of a pragmatic arrangement with a man she'd begun to realise she was half in love with but who didn't love her.

By the end of the long-haul flight to Montovia—Australia to Europe being a flight of some twenty-two hours—Eliza was avoiding Dominic as much as she could within the confines of the private jet. Andie was okay. Eliza didn't think she had a clue about how much Eliza was beginning to regret the way she had handled her relationship with Jake. But she didn't want to share those thoughts with anyone.

She hoped she and Dominic would more easily be able to steer clear of each other in the vast expanses of the royal castle. Avoiding Tristan might not be so easy.

The day after she'd landed in Montovia, Eliza sat in Gemma's exquisitely decorated office in the Crown Prince's private apartment at the castle. A 'small' room, it contained Gemma's desk and a French antique table and chairs, around which the three Party Queens were now grouped. Under the window, which looked out onto the palace gardens, there was a beautiful chaise longue that Eliza recognised from her internet video conversations with Gemma.

What a place for three ordinary Aussie girls to have ended up for a meeting, Eliza couldn't help thinking.

The three Party Queens were more subdued than usual, with the future of the company they had started more as a lark than any seriously considered business decision now under threat. It was still considered the best party planning business in Sydney, but it was at a crossroads—Eliza had been pointing that out with increasing urgency over the last months.

'I thought it would be too intimidating for us to meet in the castle boardroom,' auburn-haired Gemma explained once they were all settled. 'Even after we were married it took me a while before I could overcome my nerves enough to make a contribution there.'

Andie laughed. 'This room is so easy on the eye I might find it difficult to concentrate from being too busy admiring all the treasures.'

'Not to mention the distraction of the view out to those beautiful roses,' Eliza said.

It felt surreal to be one day in the late winter of Australia, the next day in the late summer of Europe.

'Okay, down to business,' said Gemma. 'We all know Party Queens is facing some challenges. Not least is the fact that I now live here, while the business is based in Sydney.'

'Which makes it problematical when your awesome skills with food are one of the contributing factors to our success,' said Eliza.

'True,' said Andie. 'Even as Creative Director, there are limitations to what I can do in terms of clever food ideas. Those ideas need to be validated by a food expert to tell me if they can be practical.'

Gemma nodded. 'I can still devise menus from here. And I can still test recipes myself, as I like to do.' The fact that Gemma had been testing a recipe for a white chocolate and citrus mud cake when she had first met Tristan, incognito in Sydney, had been fuel for a flurry of women's magazine articles. More so when the recipe had become the royal wedding cake. 'But the truth is both the time difference between Montovia and Sydney and my royal duties make a hands-on presence from me increasingly difficult.'

Eliza swallowed hard against a dry throat. 'Does that mean you want to resign from the partnership, Gemma?'

'Heavens, no,' said Gemma. 'But maybe I need to look at my role in a different way.'

'And then there's your future as a sole parent to consider, Eliza,' said Andie.

'Don't think I haven't thought of the challenges that will present,' Eliza said.

'Think about those challenges and multiply them a hundred times,' said Andie, and put up her hand to stop the protest Eliza was already formulating. 'Being a parent is tough, Eliza. Even tougher without a pair of loving hands from the other parent to help you out.'

Eliza gritted her teeth. She was sure Andie had meant 'the other parent' in abstract terms. But of course she could only think of Jake in that context.

'I understand that, Andie,' she said. 'And my bouts of extreme nausea showed me that even with the best workaholic will in the world there are times when the baby will have to come before the business.'

Andie raised her hand for attention. 'May I throw into the mix the fact that Dominic and I would like another baby? With two children, perhaps more, I might have to scale down my practical involvement as well.'

'It's good to have everything on the table,' said Eliza. 'No doubt a royal heir might factor into *your* future, Gemma.'

'I hope so,' said Gemma with a smile. 'We're waiting until a year after the wedding to think about that. I need to learn how to be a princess before I tackle motherhood.'

'Now we've heard the problems, I'm sure you've come armed with a plan to solve them, Eliza,' said Andie.

This kind of dilemma was something Eliza was more familiar with than the complications of her relationship with Jake. She felt very confident on this turf.

'Of course,' she said. 'The business is still very healthy, so option one is to sell Party Queens.'

She was gratified at the wails of protest from Gemma and Andie.

'It *is* a viable option,' she continued. 'There are two possible buyers—'

'No,' said Andie.

'No,' echoed Gemma.

'How could the business be the same without us?' said Andie, with an arrogant flick of her blonde-streaked hair. 'We *are* the Party Queens.'

'Good,' said Eliza. 'I feel the same way. The other proposal is to bring in another level of management in Sydney. Gemma would become a non-executive director, acting as ongoing adviser to a newly appointed food manager.'

Gemma nodded. 'Good idea. I have someone in mind. I've worked with her as a consultant and she would be ideal.'

Eliza continued. 'And Andie would train a creative person to bring on board so she can eventually work part-time. I'm thinking Jeremy.'

Freelance stylist Jeremy had been working with them since the beginning—long forgiven for his role in the disastrous Christmas tree incident that had rocked Andie and Dominic's early relationship.

Andie frowned. 'Jeremy is so talented… He's awesome. And he's really organised. But he's not a Party Queen.' She paused. 'Actually, he's a queen of a different stripe. I think he'd love to come on board.'

'Which brings us to *you*, Eliza,' said Gemma.

Eliza heaved a great sigh, reluctant to be letting go.

'I'm thinking I need to appoint a business manager to deal with the day-to-day finances and accounting.'

'Good idea.' Andie reached out a hand to take Eliza's. 'But you, out of all of us, might have a difficult time relinquishing absolute control over the business we started,' she said gently.

'I… I get that,' Eliza said.

Gemma smiled her friendship and understanding. 'Will you be able to give a manager the freedom to make decisions independent of you? Not hover over them and micro-manage them? Like watching a cake rise in the oven?'

Eliza bowed her head. 'I really am a control freak, aren't I?'

Andie squeezed her hand. 'You said it, not me.'

'I reckon your control freak tendencies are a big part of Party Queens's success,' said Gemma. 'You've really kept us on track.'

'But they could also lead to its downfall if I don't loosen the reins,' said Eliza thoughtfully.

'It's a matter of believing someone can do the job as well as you—even if they do it differently,' said Andie.

'Of accepting help because you need it,' said Gemma.

Her friends were talking about Party Queens. But, seen through the filter of her relationship with Jake, Eliza saw how she might have done things very differently. She'd fought so hard not to relinquish control over her life, over her baby—over her heart—she hadn't seen what Jake could bring to her. Not just as a father but as a life partner. Maybe she had driven him to excessive control on his side because she hadn't given an inch on hers.

In hindsight, she realised she might have thought

more about compromise than control. When it came to giving third chances, maybe it should have been *her* begging *him* for a chance to make it right.

CHAPTER FIFTEEN

DINNER AT THE royal castle of Montovia was a very formal affair. Luckily Eliza had been warned by Gemma to pack appropriate clothes. From her experiences of dinners at the castle before the wedding she knew that meant a dress that would be appropriate for a ball in Sydney. Thank heaven she still fitted into her favourite vintage ballgown in an empire style in shimmering blue that was very flattering to her pregnant shape.

Still, when she went down to dinner in the private section of the palace that was never opened to the public, she was astounded to see the level of formality of the other guests. She blinked at the dazzle of jewellery glinting in the lights from the chandeliers. It took her a moment to realise they were all members of Tristan and Gemma's bridal party. Tristan's sister Princess Natalia, his cousin with his doctor fiancée, she and Andie, other close friends of Tristan's. Natalia waved when she caught her eye.

'It's a wedding reunion,' Andie said when Eliza was seated beside her at the ornate antique banqueting table.

'So I see. Did you know about it?' Eliza asked.

'No. Gemma didn't either. Apparently when Tristan knew we were coming to visit he arranged it as a surprise¸ He invited everyone, and these are the ones who could make it. Obviously we're the only Australians.'

'What a lovely thing for him to do,' Eliza said.

Gemma was glowing with happiness.

'Very romantic,' said Andie. 'Gemma really struck husband gold with Tristan, in more ways than one.'

It was romantic in a very heart-wrenching way for Eliza. Because the most important member of the wedding party was not here—the best man, Jake.

Bittersweet memories of her last visit to the castle came flooding back in a painful rush. During the entire wedding she'd been on the edge of excitement, longing for a moment alone with him. How dismally it had all turned out. Except for the baby. Her miracle baby. Why couldn't it be enough to have the baby she'd yearned for? Why did she ache to have the father too?

What with being in a different time zone, Eliza was being affected by more than a touch of jet-lag. She also had to be careful about what she ate. The worst, most debilitating attacks of nausea seemed to have passed, but she still had to take care. She just picked at course after course of the magnificent feast—in truth she had no appetite. As soon as it was polite to do so she would make her excuses and go back up to her guest suite— the same luxurious set of rooms she'd been given on her last visit.

After dessert had been cleared Tristan asked his guests to move into the adjoining reception room, where coffee was to be served. There were gasps of surprise as the guests trooped in, at the sight of a large screen on one wall, with images of the wedding projected onto it. The guests burst into spontaneous applause.

Eliza stared at the screen. There was Gemma, getting ready with her bridesmaids. And Eliza herself, smiling as she patted a stray lock of Gemma's auburn hair back into place. The images flashed by. Andie. Natalia. The Queen placing a diamond tiara on Gemma's head.

Then there were pictures at the cathedral. The cluster of tiny flower girls. The groomsmen. The best man—Jake—standing at the altar with Tristan. Jake was smiling straight at the first bridesmaid coming up the aisle. *Her.* She was smiling back at him. It must have been so obvious to everyone what was going on between them. And here she was—without him. But pregnant with his baby.

Her hand went to her heart when she saw a close-up of Jake saying something to Tristan. The image was so large he seemed life-size. Jake looked so handsome her mouth went dry and her heart started to thud so hard she had to take deep breaths to try and control it.

She couldn't endure this. It was cruel. No one would realise if she slipped away. They were all too engrossed with the photographs.

She turned, picked up her long skirts.

And came face to face with Jake.

It was as if the image of him that had so engrossed her on the screen had come to life. Was she hallucinating? With a cautious hand, she reached out and connected with warm, solid Jake. He was real all right. She felt the colour drain from her face. He was wearing a similar tuxedo as he was in the photo, but his smile was more reticent. *He was unsure of his welcome from her.*

'Jake…' she breathed, unable to say another thing.

She felt light-headed and swayed a little. *Please. Not now.* She couldn't pass out on him again.

'You need some fresh air,' he said, and took her arm.

She let him look after her. *Liked* that he wanted to look after her. Without protest she let him lead her out of the room and then found her voice—though not any coherent words to say with it.

'What…? How…?'

'I was in London when Tristan called me about the wedding party reunion. I got here as soon as I could when I heard you were in Montovia.'

Eliza realised he was leading her onto the same terrace where they'd parted the last time they'd been in Montovia. Not quite the same view—it must be further down from that grand ballroom—and not a full moon over the lake either. But a new moon—a crescent moon that gave her a surge of hope for a new start.

She took another deep, steadying breath. Looked up at him and hoped he saw in her eyes what she was feeling but was unable to express.

'Jake, I'm asking for a third chance. Will you give it to me?'

Jake prided himself on being able to read Eliza's expressions. But he couldn't put a label on what he saw shining from her eyes. He must be reading into it what he longed to see, not what was really there. But he took hope from even that glimmering of emotion.

'Of course I give you a third chance,' he said hoarsely. He'd give her a million chances if they brought her back to him. 'But only if you'll give *me* a third chance.'

'Third chance granted,' she said, a tremulous edge to her voice.

He pulled her into his arms and held her close, breathed in her sweet scent. She slid her arms around his back and pressed closer with a little sigh. He smiled at the feel of her slender body, with the distinct curve of his baby resting under her heart. *His baby. His woman.* Now he had to convince her—not coerce her—into letting him be her man.

He looked over her head to the dark night sky, illuminated only by a sliver of silver moon, and thanked whatever power it was that had given him this chance to make good the wrongs he'd done her.

'I've missed you,' he said, not sure how to embellish his words any further.

'I've missed you too. Terribly.'

He'd flown back to Brisbane after she'd left him at the lawyer's office. His house had seemed empty—his life empty. He'd longed to be back with Eliza in her little house, with the red front door and the dragonfly doorknocker. Instead he'd tied her down to a contract to ensure his child's presence in his life and in doing so had driven her away from him.

Over and over he'd relived his time with her in Port Douglas. The passion and wonder of making love with her. Thought of the real reason he wanted to spend millions to relocate his company to Sydney. The overwhelming urge to protect her he'd felt as he'd held her hand in the ambulance and soothed her fears she might lose the baby she'd longed for. *His baby.* The incredible gift he'd been able to give her. The baby was a bonus. Eliza was the prize. But he still had to win her.

Eliza pulled away from his arms but stayed very close.

'Jake, I don't hate you—really, I don't.' The words tumbled out of her as if she had been saving them up. 'And I don't think you're a bullying thug. I... I'm really sorry I called you that.'

He'd always known he'd have to tell her the truth about his past some time—sooner rather than later. Her words seemed to be a segue into it. There was a risk that she would despise him and walk away. But he had to take that risk. If only because she was the mother of his child.

He cleared his throat. 'You're not the first person to call me a bully and a thug,' he said.

She frowned. 'What do you mean?'

'When I was fifteen years old I came up in front of the children's court and was charged with a criminal offence. The magistrate used just those words.'

'Jake!'

To his relief, there was disbelief in her voice, in the widening of her eyes, but not disgust.

'I was the leader of a gang of other young thugs. We'd stolen a car late one night and crashed it into a shopfront. I wasn't driving, but I took responsibility. The police thought it was a ram-raid—that we'd driven into the shop on purpose. In fact it was an accident. None of us could drive properly. We didn't have a driver's licence between us—we were too young. With the pumped-up pride of an adolescent male, I thought it was cooler to be charged with a ram-raid than admit to being an idiot. It was my second time before the court so I got sentenced to a spell in juvenile detention.'

Eliza kept close, didn't back away from him in horror. 'You? In a gang? I can't believe it. Why?'

'Things weren't great at home. My grandfather,

who was the only father I'd ever known, had died. My mother had a boyfriend I couldn't stand. I was angry. I was hurting. The gang was a family of sorts, and I was the kingpin.'

'Juvenile detention—that's jail, isn't it?'

'A medium security prison for kids aged from eleven to sixteen.'

She shuddered. 'I still can't believe I'm hearing this. How awful for you.'

He gritted his teeth. 'I won't lie. It *was* awful. There were some really tough kids in there.'

'Thank heaven you survived.' Her voice was warm with compassion.

She placed her hand on his cheek. He covered it with his own.

'My luck turned with the care officer assigned to me. Jim Hill. He saw I was bored witless at school and looking for diversion.'

'The school hadn't realised you were a genius?'

'They saw me as a troublemaker. Jim really helped me with anger management, with confidence-building. He showed me I had choices.' Jake smiled at the memory. 'He knew I hungered for what I didn't have, after growing up poor. Jim told me I had the brains to become a criminal mastermind or to make myself a fortune in the commercial world. The choice was mine. When my detention was over he worked with my mother to get me moved to a different school in a different area, further down the coast. The new school put me into advanced classes that challenged me. I chose to take the second path. You know the rest.'

Eliza's eyes narrowed. 'Jim Hill? The name sounds familiar.'

'He heads up The Underground Help Centre. You must have met him at the launch party.'

'So you introduced him to Dominic?'

'Jim introduced *me* to Dominic. Dominic was under his care too. But that's Dominic's story to tell. Thanks to Jim, Dominic and I already knew each other by the time we started uni. We both credit Jim for getting our lives on track. That's why we got him on board to help other young people in trouble like we were.'

'How have you managed to keep this under wraps?'

'Juvenile records are sealed when a young offender turns eighteen. I was given a fresh start and I took it. Now you know the worst about me, Eliza.'

Jake was such a tall, powerfully built man. And yet at that moment he seemed to Eliza as vulnerable as his fifteen-year-old self must have been, standing before a magistrate, waiting to hear his sentence.

She leaned up and kissed him on his cheek. It wasn't time yet for any other kind of kiss. Not until they knew where this evening might take them. Since they'd last stood on this terrace together they'd accumulated so much more baggage. Not to mention a baby bump.

'That's a story of courage and determination,' she said. 'Can you imagine if someone ever made a movie of your life story?'

'Never going to happen,' he growled.

'Well, it will make a marvellous story to tell your child one day.'

'Heavily censored,' he said, with a hint of the grin she had got so fond of.

She slowly shook her head. 'I wish you'd told me before. It helps me understand you. And I've been struggling to understand you, Jake.'

To think she had thought him superficial. He'd just been good at hiding his wounds.

He took both her hands in his and drew her closer. 'Would it have made a difference if I'd told you?'

'To help me see why you're so determined to give your child a name? Yes. To make me understand why you're so driven? Yes. To make me love you even more, knowing what you went through? Yes. And I—'

'Stop right there, Eliza,' he said, his voice hoarse. 'Did you just say you love me?'

Over the last days she'd gotten so used to thinking how much she loved him, she'd just blurted out the words. She could deny it. But what would be the point?

She looked up into his face, saw not just good looks but also his innate strength and integrity, and answered him with honesty. 'Yes, Jake, I love you. I fell in love with you... I can't think when. Yes, I can. Here. Right here on this terrace. No. Earlier than that. Actually, from the first moment. Only you weren't free. And then there was Port Douglas, and I got all tied up in not wanting to get hurt again, and...'

She realised he hadn't said anything further and began to feel exposed and vulnerable that she'd confessed she'd fallen in love with a man who had never given any indication that he might love *her*.

She tried to pull away but he kept a firm grip on her hands. 'I... I know you don't feel the same, Jake, so I—'

'What makes you say that? Of *course* I love you. I fell in love with you the first time I was best man to your bridesmaid. We must have felt it at the same moment. You in that blue bridesmaid's dress, with white flowers in your hair...'

'At Andie's wedding?' she said, shaking her head in wonder.

'At Dominic's wedding,' he said at the same time.

He drew her closer. This man who wanted to care for her, look after her, miraculously seemed to love her.

'You laughed at something I said and looked up at me with those incredible blue eyes and I fell right into them.'

'I remember that moment,' she said slowly. 'It felt like time suddenly stopped. The wedding was going on all around me, and all I could think of was how smitten I was with you.'

'But I was too damn tied up with protecting myself to let myself recognise it,' he said.

'Just as well, really,' she said. 'I wasn't ready for something so life-changing then. And you certainly weren't.'

'You could look at it that way. Or you could see that we wasted a lot of time.'

'Then the baby complicated things.'

'Yes,' he said.

The spectre of that dreadful contract hovered between them.

'Your pregnancy brought out my old fears,' he said. 'I'd chosen not to be a father because I don't know *how* to be a father. I had no role model. My uncle lived in the Northern Territory and I rarely saw him. My grandfather tried his best to be a male influence in my life but he was quite old, and suffering from the emphysema that eventually killed him.'

She nodded with realisation. 'You were *scared* to be a father.'

'I was *terrified* I'd be a bad father.'

'Do you still think that way?'

'Not so much.'

'Why?'

'Because of you,' he said. 'I know you're going to be a brilliant mother, Eliza. That will help me to be the best father I can be to our child.'

'Thank you for the vote of confidence,' she said a little shakily. 'But I'll have to *learn* to be a mother. We'll *both* have to learn to be parents. And I know our daughter will have the most wonderful daddy who—'

'Our *daughter*?'

Eliza snatched her hand to her mouth. 'I haven't had a chance to tell you. I had another ultrasound last week.'

For the first time Jake placed his hand reverently on her bump. 'A little girl…' he said, his voice edged with awe. 'My daughter.'

For a long moment Eliza looked up at Jake, taking in the wonder and anticipation on his face.

'So…so where does that leave us?' she asked finally.

'I'm withdrawing my offer of marriage,' he said.

'*What?*'

Jake looked very serious. 'It was more a command than a proposal. I want to do it properly.'

'Do *what* properly?'

But she thought she might know what. Hope flew into her mind like a tiny bird and flew frantically around, trilling to be heard.

'Propose,' he said.

Jake cradled her face in his big, strong hands. His green eyes looked intently down into hers.

'Eliza, I love you. Will you marry me? Do me the honour of becoming my wife?'

She didn't hesitate. 'Yes, Jake, yes. Nothing would make me happier than to be your wife. I love you.'

Now was the time to kiss. He gathered her into his arms and claimed her mouth. She wound her arms around his neck and kissed him back, her heart singing with joy. She loved him and she wanted him and now he was hers. No way would she be alone in that palatial guest apartment tonight.

Jake broke away from the kiss. Then came back for another brief kiss, as if he couldn't get enough of her. He reached inside his jacket to an inside pocket. Then pulled out a small embossed leather box and flipped it open.

Eliza was too stunned to say anything, to do anything other than stare at the huge, perfect solitaire diamond on a fine platinum band, glinting in the faint silver light of the new moon. He picked up her hand and slipped the ring onto the third finger of her left hand. It fitted perfectly.

'I love it,' she breathed. 'Where did you get—?'

'In London.'

'But—'

'I was planning to propose in Sydney. But then Tristan invited me here.'

'Back to where it started.'

He kissed her again, a kiss that was tender and loving and full of promise.

'Can we get married as soon as possible?' he asked.

She paused. 'For the baby's sake?'

'To make you my wife and me your husband. This is about us committing to each other, Eliza. Not because you're pregnant. The baby is a happy bonus.'

'So what happens about the contract once we're married?'

'That ill-conceived contract? After I left you at the elevator I went back to the meeting room and tore my copy up. Then I fired my lawyer for giving me such bad advice.'

She laughed. 'I put my copy through the shredder.'

'We'll be brilliant parents without any need for that,' he said.

'I love you, Jake,' she said, rejoicing in the words, knowing she would be saying them over and over again in the years to come.

'I love you too, Eliza.' He lowered his head to kiss her again.

'Eliza, are you okay? We were worried—'

Andie's voice made both Eliza and Jake turn.

'Oh,' said Andie. Then, *'Oh...'* again, in a very knowing way.

Gemma was there too. She smiled. 'I can see you're okay.'

'Very okay,' Eliza said, smiling her joy. She held out her left hand and splayed her fingers, the better to display her ring. 'We're engaged. For real engaged.'

Andie and Gemma hugged her and Jake, accompanying their hugs with squeals of excitement and delight. Then Dominic and Tristan were there, slapping Jake on the back and hugging her, telling her they were glad she'd come to her senses and that they hoped she realised what a good man she'd got.

'Oh, I realise, all right,' she said, looking up at Jake.

'I couldn't think of a better man to be my husband and the father of my child.'

'You got the best man,' said Jake with a grin.

CHAPTER SIXTEEN

THE BEAUTY OF having your own party planning business, Eliza mused, was that it was possible to organise a wedding in two weeks flat without cutting any corners.

Everything was perfect, she thought with satisfaction on the afternoon of her wedding day. They'd managed to keep her snaring of 'the Billionaire Bachelor' under the media radar. So she and Jake were getting the quiet, intimate wedding they both wanted without any intrusion from the press.

It had been quite a feat to keep it quiet. After all, not only was the most eligible bachelor in Australia getting married, but the guest list of close family and friends included royalty.

Andie had found a fabulous waterfront house at Kirribilli as their venue. The weather was perfect, and the ceremony was to be held on the expansive lawns that stretched right down to the harbour wall, with the Opera House and Sydney Harbour Bridge as backdrop.

It really was just as she wanted it, Eliza thought as she stood with her father at the end of the veranda. Andie had arranged two rows of elegant white bamboo chairs to form an aisle. Large white metal vases filled with informal bunches of white flowers marked the end of each row of seats.

Now, the chairs were all filled with guests, heads turned, waiting for the bride to make her entrance. Everyone she cared about was there, including Jake's mother, whom she'd liked instantly.

Ahead, Jake stood flanked by his best man, Dominic, and his groomsman Tristan, at one side of the simple white wedding arch completely covered in white flowers where the celebrant waited. On the other side stood her bridesmaids, Andie and Gemma. A jazz band played softly. When it struck up the chords of the traditional 'Wedding March', it was Eliza's cue to head down the aisle. On the back of a white pony named Molly—her father's wedding gift to her.

Her vintage-inspired, full-skirted tea-length gown hadn't really been chosen with horseback-riding in mind. But when her father had reminded her of how as a little girl she had always wanted to ride to her wedding on her pony, she had fallen for the idea. Andie had had hysterics, but eventually caved in.

'I really hope we can carry this off, Dad,' Eliza said now, as her father helped her up into the side saddle.

'Of course you can, love,' he said. 'You're still the best horsewoman I know.'

Amazing how a wedding and a baby could bring families together, she thought. Her father had mellowed and their rift had been healed—much to her mother's joy. Now Eliza was seated on Molly and her father was leading the pony by a lead-rope entwined with white ribbons down the grassy aisle. There was no 'giving away' of the bride as part of the ceremony. She and Jake were giving themselves to each other.

Her entrance was met with surprised delight and the sound of many cameras clicking.

Jake didn't know about her horseback entrance—she'd kept it a secret. 'Brilliant,' he whispered as he helped her off Molly and into his arms. 'Country girl triumphs.'

But once the novelty of her entrance was over, and her father had led Molly away, it was all about Jake and her.

They had written the words of the ceremony themselves, affirming their love and respect for each other and their commitment to a lifetime together as well as their anticipation of being parents. Her dress did nothing to disguise her bump—she hadn't wanted to hide the joyous presence of their miracle baby.

Everything around her seemed to recede as she exchanged her vows with Jake, looking up into his face, his eyes never leaving hers. Their first kiss as husband and wife went on for so long their friends starting applauding.

'I love you,' she whispered, just for his ears.

'For always and for ever,' he whispered back.

* * * * *

MILLS & BOON®
Hardback – July 2016

ROMANCE

Di Sione's Innocent Conquest	Carol Marinelli
Capturing the Single Dad's Heart	Kate Hardy
The Billionaire's Ruthless Affair	Miranda Lee
A Virgin for Vasquez	Cathy Williams
Master of Her Innocence	Chantelle Shaw
Moretti's Marriage Command	Kate Hewitt
The Flaw in Raffaele's Revenge	Annie West
The Unwanted Conti Bride	Tara Pammi
Bought by Her Italian Boss	Dani Collins
Wedded for His Royal Duty	Susan Meier
His Cinderella Heiress	Marion Lennox
The Bridesmaid's Baby Bump	Kandy Shepherd
Bound by the Unborn Baby	Bella Bucannon
Taming Hollywood's Ultimate Playboy	Amalie Berlin
Winning Back His Doctor Bride	Tina Beckett
White Wedding for a Southern Belle	Susan Carlisle
Wedding Date with the Army Doc	Lynne Marshall
The Baby Inheritance	Maureen Child
Expecting the Rancher's Child	Sara Orwig
Doctor, Mummy...Wife?	Dianne Drake

MILLS & BOON®
Large Print – July 2016

ROMANCE

The Italian's Ruthless Seduction	Miranda Lee
Awakened by Her Desert Captor	Abby Green
A Forbidden Temptation	Anne Mather
A Vow to Secure His Legacy	Annie West
Carrying the King's Pride	Jennifer Hayward
Bound to the Tuscan Billionaire	Susan Stephens
Required to Wear the Tycoon's Ring	Maggie Cox
The Greek's Ready-Made Wife	Jennifer Faye
Crown Prince's Chosen Bride	Kandy Shepherd
Billionaire, Boss...Bridegroom?	Kate Hardy
Married for Their Miracle Baby	Soraya Lane

HISTORICAL

The Secrets of Wiscombe Chase	Christine Merrill
Rake Most Likely to Sin	Bronwyn Scott
An Earl in Want of a Wife	Laura Martin
The Highlander's Runaway Bride	Terri Brisbin
Lord Crayle's Secret World	Lara Temple

MEDICAL

A Daddy for Baby Zoe?	Fiona Lowe
A Love Against All Odds	Emily Forbes
Her Playboy's Proposal	Kate Hardy
One Night...with Her Boss	Annie O'Neil
A Mother for His Adopted Son	Lynne Marshall
A Kiss to Change Her Life	Karin Baine

MILLS & BOON®
Hardback – August 2016

ROMANCE

The Di Sione Secret Baby	Maya Blake
Carides's Forgotten Wife	Maisey Yates
The Playboy's Ruthless Pursuit	Miranda Lee
His Mistress for a Week	Melanie Milburne
Crowned for the Prince's Heir	Sharon Kendrick
In the Sheikh's Service	Susan Stephens
Marrying Her Royal Enemy	Jennifer Hayward
Claiming His Wedding Night	Louise Fuller
An Unlikely Bride for the Billionaire	Michelle Douglas
Falling for the Secret Millionaire	Kate Hardy
The Forbidden Prince	Alison Roberts
The Best Man's Guarded Heart	Katrina Cudmore
Seduced by the Sheikh Surgeon	Carol Marinelli
Challenging the Doctor Sheikh	Amalie Berlin
The Doctor She Always Dreamed Of	Wendy S. Marcus
The Nurse's Newborn Gift	Wendy S. Marcus
Tempting Nashville's Celebrity Doc	Amy Ruttan
Dr White's Baby Wish	Sue MacKay
For Baby's Sake	Janice Maynard
An Heir for the Billionaire	Kat Cantrell

MILLS & BOON®
Large Print – August 2016

ROMANCE

The Sicilian's Stolen Son	Lynne Graham
Seduced into Her Boss's Service	Cathy Williams
The Billionaire's Defiant Acquisition	Sharon Kendrick
One Night to Wedding Vows	Kim Lawrence
Engaged to Her Ravensdale Enemy	Melanie Milburne
A Diamond Deal with the Greek	Maya Blake
Inherited by Ferranti	Kate Hewitt
The Billionaire's Baby Swap	Rebecca Winters
The Wedding Planner's Big Day	Cara Colter
Holiday with the Best Man	Kate Hardy
Tempted by Her Tycoon Boss	Jennie Adams

HISTORICAL

The Widow and the Sheikh	Marguerite Kaye
Return of the Runaway	Sarah Mallory
Saved by Scandal's Heir	Janice Preston
Forbidden Nights with the Viscount	Julia Justiss
Bound by One Scandalous Night	Diane Gaston

MEDICAL

His Shock Valentine's Proposal	Amy Ruttan
Craving Her Ex-Army Doc	Amy Ruttan
The Man She Could Never Forget	Meredith Webber
The Nurse Who Stole His Heart	Alison Roberts
Her Holiday Miracle	Joanna Neil
Discovering Dr Riley	Annie Claydon

MILLS & BOON®

Why shop at millsandboon.co.uk?

Each year, thousands of romance readers find their perfect read at millsandboon.co.uk. That's because we're passionate about bringing you the very best romantic fiction. Here are some of the advantages of shopping at www.millsandboon.co.uk:

* **Get new books first**—you'll be able to buy your favourite books one month before they hit the shops

* **Get exclusive discounts**—you'll also be able to buy our specially created monthly collections, with up to 50% off the RRP

* **Find your favourite authors**—latest news, interviews and new releases for all your favourite authors and series on our website, plus ideas for what to try next

* **Join in**—once you've bought your favourite books, don't forget to register with us to rate, review and join in the discussions

Visit **www.millsandboon.co.uk**
for all this and more today!